The Journey to the Giants

By Stephen John Beccia

Treelanders

First Printing June 2010

ISBN 978-0-9824331-3-3

Written by Stephen Beccia

Cover by Windward Design

Published by Dailey Swan Publishing, Inc

Dailey Swan Publishing, Inc
2644 Appian Way #101
Pinole Ca 94564
www.Daileyswanpublishing.com

This book is dedicated to: Caitlyn, Emelia, Willow, Avry, and Trueman.
You are my true heroes and the loves of my life.
This is where the journey begins...

Love,
Dad

For my family and friends, thanks for all your love and support.
And to Lori, thanks for your unconditional friendship.

Contents

Prologue
Dream-Demon

The dream-demon waited in darkness, and the Treelander approached. Avry Blain fell from his world full of peace and harmony and watched his fields of hidden magic melt away. The soothing aroma of pine grew musty and turned his stomach sour. There was no sign of his familiar existence, just darkness.

A mystical, cloud-covered island known as Epalushia floated through the galaxy, and traveled along the belt of the Milky Way. Upon this hovering island in the sky, nestled in the thick of a pine tree forest, the village of Treeland stood peacefully. Villagers built wooden huts and bamboo streets high upon the treetops—ancient skyscrapers where Avry and his family lived and serendipity waited in the wings.

The mysterious and faraway planet of Epalushia was also the dwelling for many other walks of life—from snot-nosed kids to royalty and some evil creatures in between—and even as it may be, Avry Blain was deep asleep and running—running through his dreams and very much *not* at peace. His body was covered in sweat, and his heart pounded like a big bass drum. For months, the young Treelander's dreams had been haunted by disturbing images—images he later would not recall, leaving him troubled and uneasy. His mother had assured him that the "dreams would soon pass" and it was only his "becoming of age" that had him troubled.

The Treelanders have an uncanny ability to travel through the forest. Using their freakishly long arms and legs, they can climb like monkeys in the jungle. Small, web-like wings sprawl under their arms like prehistoric birds and help them soar through the air to the unknown. But within Avry's dreams, he could not move. The dream-demon had the boy trapped in its tangled web and was tantalizing him with evil. Avry reached for his sword, but it was not there. Instead, the metal blade lay on his bedroom floor next to his bow and arrows. His weapons would not reach him—not until the Treelander could open his weary eyes.

Avry's long dreadlocks clung to his sweat-soaked face. Tears streamed down his olive-green cheeks. His brown peasant garments stretched and tore while he tossed in his sleep. The demon of darkness had stolen his oxygen and drowned him in fear. He could not escape the overwhelming spiders of horror that crept through his nerves.

And then, in an instant, the dream had passed, though the terror lingered. Avry's mind soared elsewhere, somewhere closer to home—Treeland—where the Treelanders were great craftsmen and hunters. They built weapons and armor for King Oliver of Epalushia. The villagers prepared food for a great feast at the king's castle and traveled to Market Square, where people throughout the land bartered and shopped.

And dreaming even deeper...Avry's mind carried him on.

Jars full of fireflies lit the streets and huts at night like natural lamps gleaming with wonder. They brightened the humble village of Treeland in a festive display. Families reunited and celebrated. Children ran and played. And after all the work was done for that day, the colony gathered around the great campfire in the village square, where a Treelander was chosen to read a story from the *Tree of Life*. Avry's disturbed mind went blank, his dreams were forgotten, his body relaxed, and a new day was born.

Chapter 1
Treat for a King

Lorri Blain scurried through the streets of Treeland village. Her alarming voice turned heads as she passed by. "Avry! Trueman! Where are they now?" she puffed. Beads of sweat ran down her flushed cheeks, and her head whipped left to right, looking down alleyways as she went.

Another woman pushing a fruit cart stopped, turned toward the lunatic mother, and inquired, "Is everything okay, Lorri?"

Lorri, the mother of five young Treelanders, was often seen running after at least one of her children. With bewildered eyes she snapped coldly, "It's not going to be if my boys are not on the hunt by now." Then she turned and stormed away.

Another hot summer had come to an end in the tiny forest of Treeland. Hunting was in full swing. Naturally, autumn was the best time to stock up food for the long, harsh winter. Wild burlybeast would soon migrate into the mountains before the caves iced over and the lakes turned into frigid cakes. Only the strong pine trees carried a green luster year round, while the oaks and maples shed their multicolored coats.

The scent of pine, fir, and honeysuckle tickled the air as the Treelanders muddled about their wooden village doing early morning chores. The natural aroma kept the mood cheerful even during extremely laborious tasks. And while the day had begun for most, two boys remained to be seen.

Avry and his younger brother, Trueman, were inside their cluttered bedroom hut, sunk in their hammocks, discussing the day's upcoming events. Avry boasted to Trueman that he would take the trophy in the fencing contest. "The prince's sword is no match against mine. I guarantee you that," he ranted.

"Well, I'm sure that I'll win the knapsack race, hands down," Trueman boasted.

"I don't see why not...you've only been practicing for three months," Avry snickered.

"Are you going to enter the fishing contest too?" Trueman asked.

"Only if I can fix my reel before the tournament," Avry said. "The box trout that I snagged last week snapped my line and jammed up the works."

There was no hint of the real adventure in store as they continued their conversation. Magic and evil lurked down their future path, and destiny would lead the way—the way that began over the treetops and led up to the mountains, where *something* lurked within the darkness. *Its* eyes stared down upon the green forest that was filled with life. The bitter *soul* hated them all—the Treelanders, King Oliver, and the Epalushia kingdom. No one was aware of *its* menacing presence. Not yet anyway. The *dark* stranger's stone-like face and venomous demon eyes grew wild as evil brewed inside its head. *Its* supernatural ears listened into the forest when a mother Treelander called to her boys.

"Avry and Trueman…stop lying around and get out here this instant!" The boys jumped up as she continued, "You know today is a big day, and we have to get ready for King Oliver's birthday celebration. Hurry up, time's a wasting!" She watched them as they sprang out of their huts in a mad rush. Their hair was still mangled, and their shirts were wrinkled and twisted.

"Now run off and catch a burlybeast, would you?" She continued, "And don't be back late!" The morning sun made her auburn hair glow like a lighted torch, and her striking emerald green eyes gleamed brightly as she looked upon her boys.

Trueman, the youngest of the Treelanders, was a small and timid boy, with a round face and long black hair. He stuck like glue to Avry's side and was the most curious of the bunch. "B-b-burlybeast?" Trueman quivered. His blue eyes popped wide open.

"Yes!" their mother insisted. "Your sisters are already on their way to the castle with the new crown that your father crafted for the king, and you only have a few hours."

The boys were already halfway down a tree and on their way to the burlybeast field when Avry shouted, "Okay, Mum!"

She barely heard his reply but knew that her boys were always eager to hunt. Or, at least Avry was. As for Trueman, he was still trying to get the hang of it.

Avry and Trueman jumped from tree to tree, slid up and down branches, and swung off of tree vines like monkeys. Within minutes they reached a clearing in the forest where they heard the grunts of the untamed burlybeasts.

"I don't like burlybeasts," Trueman said.

"Don't worry, just stay behind me and do what I say and you'll be fine," Avry said as he pointed to the ground behind him with great command.

The boys ducked down behind a red berry bush and watched the burlybeasts graze in the plush, green field of grass and flowers. Avry reached slowly for his bow and arrow then aimed straight at the biggest beast in the bunch. Large black eyes peeked through the long, scraggly, gray hair that covered the beast's body.

Avry whispered to himself, "Hold it right there." With one eye squinted he looked down the shaft of the arrow. The beast shook its head full of white spiked horns and snorted.

"Shouldn't you use your sword?" Trueman asked.

"No. This will be easier. Just watch."

Without warning, Trueman became startled when he felt the clammy nose of a burlybeast on his back. The beast snorted and grunted from an unpleasant aroma. Trueman grabbed his sword, swung it in the air, screamed at the top of his lungs, and ran at the flock of burlybeasts.

"What are ya doin'?" Avry hollered, his mouth stuck open, and his bottom lip quaking.

But it was too late. Avry's screams of disbelief did not help, and the flock of burlybeasts screeched while they ran in every direction. It wasn't until they were gone into the thick of the forest that Avry said, "Thought that would work better, did ya, Trueman?" He scowled and crossed his arms.

Trueman stood in the empty field with his hands cupped to his mouth and began to shout, "Come back! Wait...please...come... back!"

"Well, that's just great!" Avry sighed and put an arrow against his head. "Mum and Dad are gonna kill us if we don't bring back a beast."

"M-ma-maybe we can go to Market Square and buy one," Trueman said, his voice trembling.

Avry escalated his taunts, "Market Square...Market Square! Let's see, we hunted for the past week, caught thirty burlybeasts, sold them to Market Square, and now you want to go buy them back?" Breathing heavily, he paused and thought for a moment before he asked, "Trueman, did you bring any treasures with ya?"

"Nope, just my wooden flute."

"That might buy us a trip to the King's dungeon. We need something good to trade at the Square, not your silly flute."

Avry's tall, lanky body swayed back and forth. He stood deep in thought with his arms crossed and his eyes fixed on his brother. His dark brown eyes were mesmerizing; they gazed upon Trueman and slowly hypnotized him.

Avry loved his little brother; he knew they would need to think of something creative to keep them out of trouble. He paused for a long time while Trueman sat by him quietly and then an idea shot through his brain like lightning, "I've got it! Let's go to Sky Lake and catch some gold flakes beneath the Great Falls." The idea wasn't up for discussion. The anxious boys hurried off without another word.

Sky Lake was covered in a ghostly cloud of mist from the huge waterfall that dumped into it. The nearby mountain spiked straight up and surrounded the lake like a giant horseshoe. The Great Falls poured down the middle of the jagged rocks and grass sprouted from the many cracks and crevasses.

Within minutes, the boys arrived at the lake and were in good spirits. They hoped they would find the precious golden flakes. They walked along the pebble beach at the basin of the Great Falls and approached the clear shimmering water. Even though it took most miners a good week's worth of digging to find their riches, Avry and Trueman stretched their hands down to the bottom of the water and prayed for instant glory. They clawed at the gritty bottom and pulled up fists filled with muck. Avry inspected the muck carefully only to find sand, weeds, and no golden flakes.

Trueman plunged his hands back in the water and began to pull on something solid, "I think I've got one..." he said anxiously.

Snap!

Trueman went straight down on his bottom. The young Treelander giggled. He sat there for a moment with a black rock in his hand and stared up at the crisp, blue sky. Slowly he glanced downward and noticed something shining from the side of the cliff. "Avry...look!" he shouted.

Avry grabbed his looking glass (a rusty brown

tube with glass at both ends) from his dingy old backpack and aimed it at the shining object. His mouth opened wide with excitement, and he said, "It looks like a pile of treasure!"

The boys ran to the side of the cliff and began to climb the steep hill. They pulled their way up through the rocks and twigs until they reached a huge rock that jutted outward. A large straw nest lay comfortably upon the cliff; inside the nest rested an egg that sparkled with vibrant color. The oversized egg was covered with beautiful gold and diamond spots from head to toe. It was a breathtaking sight and far too irresistible for the two curious boys who jumped inside the nest for a better look.

"This will pay for a hundred burlybeasts," Trueman shouted.

"Yeah, but it must belong to somebody or something—"

"We need it!" Trueman said abruptly, and then he proceeded to roll the egg to the edge of the nest.

Avry felt an unpleasant presence, and the hair on the back of his neck stood up. With every inch that they rolled the egg, a soft thumping grew louder. A warm breeze carried an unfamiliar smell, like rotten meat mixed with rancid ocean air. Small rocks trickled down from the cliff edge above.

"I don't like the feel of this, Trueman."

The thumps rumbled louder and faster.

"What's that sound?" Trueman asked, and then answered, "Thunder?"

A large object suddenly shadowed the boys and

doused the daylight. Then, from out of the shadows came a large green flying creature that swooped down and howled at the boys. They had heard of the legend, but never had they seen such a monster up close—pointed ears, red eyes, sharp teeth, long spiked scaly tail, and large bat-like wings. It could only be one thing.

"Dragon!" Avry and Trueman yelled together.

The egg slipped from the boys' sweaty hands, and it rolled down the cliff and into the water below. Their stomachs grew nauseous, and the frightened boys watched helplessly as the egg plunged into the lake. It bobbed up and down for a second, until two unusual-looking claws reached up and pulled it below the water's surface.

Trueman and Avry slid down the steep cliff, ducking and dodging several times from the fire that spewed from the dragon's mouth. The dragon flapped its huge flesh-like wings and clawed at the ground while the boys hid behind a huge rock. The fire-breathing predator seemed heartless, just dying for vengeance. It opened its huge claws, reached for the boys, and raked at their clothes. Avry and Trueman screamed when they felt the grip of the monster squeeze tightly around their arms. Their hearts pounded hard in their chests. The enraged dragon dragged the boys across the ground until a firm voice disrupted the attack.

Chapter 2
A Dragon Tale

"Stop!" shouted an old man. He was dressed in a long black robe and held a wooden staff aimed at the sky. His face was hard to see from under the long white beard, and a black pointed hat hung over his rather big nose. "Jewlz, that's enough," he said. "You've made these green boys turn white," he paused, patted the dragon's head, and spoke softly, "Rest, my old friend."

The dragon grunted and backed away from the boys, revealing their frightened faces to the man. The stranger looked at Avry and Trueman, and chuckled, "Don't be alarmed boys. Jewlz's bite is bigger than—well, that is to say—err—uh—anyway, where was I? Oh yes...the name is Zita, wizard and keeper of this here dragon."

The dragon wandered into the shade under an oak tree, then rested her head. She snorted a few times, and then settled down to sleep.

"We meant no harm," Avry said.

The wizard ignored the boys for a minute while he walked around and mumbled to himself. He looked confused and didn't make any sense when he spoke. He was babbling in a different language, softly.

Zita scratched his head while he looked at the boys and then turned toward the lake, saying, "Hmm." The dragon let out a heavy sigh, while Zita looked up at the dragon nest and then back toward the lake. "Hmm…Well then…um…well, that is to say—ZIA!" Zita summoned.

The boys looked confused. A puff of smoke billowed from the ground, and a very short witch, all dressed in white, walked out of the cloud, "What is it now, Zita?"

"Boys, this is my twin sister, Zia. She is the problem solver in my family," Zita said.

"Well, all I can smell is sea monkeys," Zia said in a raspy quiver, "and I don't see an egg shining up in the nest. This can mean only one thing—trouble."

"We didn't know it was an egg, honest," Trueman uttered then shrugged his shoulders.

"It's not just any old egg, ya know. It's the last of its kind," Zia said, and then continued, "That egg was the last of the dragons. Jewlz is the mother, but she is very old, and dying. That egg is the beginning of new hope for our land. You see, this land is protected by the dragon, and that is why we live in peace. That is to say, as long as old Jewlz here is alive to protect us."

"Protect us from what?" Avry asked.

"A long time ago, long before you boys were born, before the Treelanders were around, everyone in the land of Epalushia was tormented by giants and treated like slaves until the dragons came along and protected the people."

"We've read the story about giants at our village, but I thought the giants were all dead and gone," Avry said.

"No, my dear," Zia replied shaking her head,

"the giants are very much alive in the forbidden land, and up until now, not one unwanted creature has ever stepped a foot into the kingdom of Epalushia while our dragon was here to protect us."

"You mean a g-g-giant was here today?" Trueman quivered.

"No, that was Raider," Zita replied. "He is an evil sea monkey who works for the giants. It was he who came here today and snatched the egg."

"That greedy, mixed up, sea monkey of a pirate. He will stop at nothing to get gold and treasure from all over the land," Zia said as her face turned scarlet.

"So Raider thought the egg was a treasure just like we did?" Avry asked.

Zia's eyes squinted as she looked out over the lake. She cleared her raspy throat and replied, "Raider has been stealing gold, diamonds, jewels, and anything that he could sell to the giants, and in return, Raider and his family live free like kings, while the giants hoard all the gold and use it to build everything that they own, even their castle."

"Yes, but soon the giants will have the egg, and that will be the end of this peaceful world as we know it," Zita sighed.

Suddenly there was a sound from the distance.

HAOOOOOOOOO!

HAOOOOOOOOOO!

The dragon quickly jumped to her feet and took off into the air. She began screeching and flew toward the bellowing sound.

"That's the warning horn at our village. Let's go, Trueman!" Avry cried.

The boys ran quickly toward their village, climbing and swinging though trees until they reached the tallest tree they could find and then jumped out into the whirling breeze. They spread their web-like wings and soared through the air like giant birds. Screams of terror grew louder as the boys approached Treeland. The only visible sight was the dragon diving through the air and spitting out fire. The boys flapped their wings with long strides and raced toward their village.

Suddenly, there was silence instead of the warning horn. The dragon had stopped screeching, and the whispering wind was all the boys could hear when they glided into Treeland.

The dragon, Zita, and Zia were standing next to a creature lying on the ground below the village. Avry and Trueman approached like birds of prey.

"What is it? Is it...dead?" Trueman asked cautiously.

"This is...err...um...was...Create, the gargoyle. He was a scout for the giants. He was after something—but what?" Zita pondered. He paused and lifted his hat to reveal his eyes, "I'm afraid we are too late, though...he has already done his damage."

"What do you mean?" Avry demanded.

"It won't be easy for you to see, but the gargoyle has cast an unspeakable curse that I must actually speak of...that is to say, if you must know."

"Yes, Zita, please, what is it?" Avry begged.

Zita looked grim and Zia bowed her head, explaining, "It is the curse of fire and ice. Your people have been turned to frightful statues. They burn now like flaming statues, and if they are not cured soon...very soon, I must add, they will turn to statues of ice, and I'm afraid to say...they will remain like that for eternity."

"Can't you use your magic and turn them back to normal?" Avry snapped. He tried to smile and hide his ill feelings, but the smile quickly turned to a frown.

"Well, it's not as easy as waving a wand, you know," Zia said.

From the deepest part of the forest came shrills of horror, as three silhouetted figures approached. It was the boys' sisters, Caitlyn, Emelia, and Willow, who had just returned from the king's castle. Caitlyn, the oldest sister, had her sword in hand, and was the first to arrive.

"We heard the horns and got here as fast as we could. What happened, and who are these people?" Caitlyn panted, wiping her blond hair from her face. She wheezed, trying hard to catch her breath, and still she asked more questions faster than they could be answered. "Where's Mom? Where's Dad? Are you guys alright?"

"Caitlyn, enough with all the questions. You sound like Trueman," Avry said as he put his long arms around Caitlyn.

Trueman just grumbled, gave Avry a nudge on his arm, and joined in the hug.

When Willow and Emelia arrived, they quickly climbed up the pine trees to the village above and searched for their parents. The girls shrieked at the sight of the villagers frozen in place like statues, and burning like large torches. Beneath the flames that crawled over their bodies, their skin had turned gray and their eyes were as black as coal. The flaming statues had not burned anything around them; the fire just crept along their bodies like slithering snakes and crackled like burning wood.

Emelia's bright green eyes filled with tears when she saw her mother. She had been repairing a necklace that Emelia had broken earlier that morning, and now she sat stone-solid in a chair, stopped in her work. Her father, Stephen, a very tall and strong man, had his sword raised to the sky like he was about to strike at something. Willow was overcome with anger and let out a primal scream while she smashed her sword into a street cart full of fruit.

"Avry! Trueman! Come quick!" Willow yelled.

Everyone had gone up to Treeland to see what the gargoyle had done to the villagers. Jewlz flew overhead to watch for any other unwanted creatures.

"D-does it hurt them?...The fire I mean," Willow asked with tears streaming down her cheeks.

"No, my dear, they feel nothing," Zia replied.

"If you're a witch and you're a wizard, then why is it that you can't turn our people back to normal?" Willow lashed out hastily. This was an uncharacteristic tone for the young teenage girl with the silky blonde hair, almond-shaped brown eyes, and soft, creamy complexion. She was the one with the warm heart, funny sense of humor, and a personality that made people smile like when they eat apple pie. Her soft, raspy voice was never angry and always had a gentle way of letting down the many unwanted boys who asked her to the Treeland Ball every spring. Her heart belonged to Peter Boland, but that never seemed to stop the other boys from asking her, just the same. But none of this mattered now. She stood sobbing, her face scarlet. Her world as she knew it had just been turned upside down.

Zia looked at Willow with a very disappointed expression and pulled out a tiny brown bottle from her pocket. The Treelanders stared at Zia with hopeful expressions and baited breath. Zia pulled the cork out of the bottle and then turned it upside down.

"Just as I thought..." said Zia. "I'm all out of giant swamp water. Sorry, kids, but without this potion there is nothing I can do."

The Treelanders let out a heavy sigh of disappointment.

"Well now, there is only one thing to do," Zita said. "You kids get your things together for a trip. There have been too many creatures from the forbidden land here today. You must get that egg and some of that giant swamp water."

"What egg, and why can't you go?" Willow asked.

"We'd love to come along but we must stay here and take care of Jewlz. Your brothers can explain the egg thing, and with all this talk you are running out of time. Meet us down by the lake when you are ready."

A blinding flash of light surrounded the wizard and witch. Within a split second they were gone.

While the Treelanders packed for their journey, Avry and Trueman explained everything about the dragon and the egg to their sisters. They all took one last look at their village where everything was standing still, and then they quickly rushed toward the woods that led to Sky Lake.

Chapter 3
The Starlight Map

It was just about sunset when the Treelanders met the witch and wizard down by the lake. A heavy mist hovered over the water, and it appeared as if Zita and Zia were walking on a cloud.

The dragon was perched in her empty nest, high on the steep cliff, overlooking the Treelanders. The Treelanders gazed out onto the lake. Their father once told them to never pass the stone arch that leads to the sea and the forbidden land.

"I don't know about this," Emelia said with some hesitation.

"Well, I don't think Mom and Dad would be happy as flaming statues or ice sculptures forever," Willow said harshly.

"No, no, Willow. I was talking about my supply of treats that I packed for the trip. You know my sugar leaves...and barking chocolates...and..."

"Enough, you two, give us a break!" Avry barked.

"We love you, too, Avry," Willow taunted, while she and Emelia laughed behind Avry's back.

Caitlyn walked to the edge of the lake where Zia and Zita stood holding hands with their eyes closed. Zia smiled at Caitlyn's presence, "Stand back, missy, you're in for a big surprise."

Caitlyn and the others stepped back. A loud, bubbling sound erupted from the lake, the wind began to blow wildly, the trees shook so hard that the tops almost touched the ground, and then something huge began to rise out of the water—a sea vessel, a long, tall, wooden sea vessel with bright red sails, cannons mounted on the side, and a small wooden plank that stretched from the ship's deck to the edge of the lake. The Treelanders were amazed at the sight. They were even more amazed when their bags and supplies levitated off the ground and flew onto the ship.

Zita greeted the kids as they approached, "Good luck, my friends, on your journey ahead. This ship is one of the fastest in the land and will help you catch up to Raider and his pathetic bunch of sea monkeys."

"Great, there's more than one sea monkey," Emelia muttered.

"How will we know which one is Raider?" Caitlyn asked.

"Well, if you two would let me finish," Zita griped. "You can't miss the horrible stench of seaweed when you get close to Raider. But just in case your noses aren't working, look for his big green teeth, bug-like red eyes, and, most distinctly, his orange spiked hair."

"I don't think I'm looking forward to this trip," Trueman whined.

Zia approached Avry and handed him a brown potion bottle, saying, "Just fill it up with the swamp water outside the giant's castle and bring it back to me. I'll fix up a potion that will cure your people, rest assured."

Avry took the bottle and put it in his backpack.

He gave Zia a hug before he stepped onto the ship with the others.

Just as Trueman and Avry were pulling up the anchors, a group of the king's knights came galloping down to the lake on big white horses.

"Stop!" shouted one of the knights. "King Oliver wanted you to have this starlight map. If you get lost, just hold it up to the stars, and it will help you find your way through the forbidden land."

The knight handed the map to Avry, turned without looking back, and galloped away with the rest of the knights.

"Ah...thanks," Avry said, even though the knights were already out of hearing range. Then he added, "That was kind of strange."

"Those knights are so mysterious; how did they know where we are going?" Caitlyn pondered.

"Yeah, and they didn't even bring any of the king's chocolate..."

"Okay, Emelia, that's enough with all the sweet-talk!" Avry shouted.

The Treelanders waved good-bye to Zia and Zita while the tall ship sailed toward a large stone archway. Once again Zia and Zita vanished into thin air, leaving Jewlz up in her nest to watch the Treelanders sail out to the sea.

Just as the ship passed into the forbidden sea, an eerie chill ran through Willow's spine. She walked to the back of the ship and noticed a dark figure peering out of the woods near the stone arch.

"Look!" Willow cried.

Caitlyn ran to the back of the ship at the shrill

of her sister's scream.

"What is it—a spider?" Caitlyn knew Willow was dreadfully scared of spiders.

"No. Some creepy man all dressed in black was staring at me."

"Well, there's nothing there," Caitlyn said. "You're just imagining things."

"I think he was trying to tell me something," Willow replied. "His mouth was moving up and down and..."

Caitlyn nudged Willow's shoulder, started to walk away, and then turned around. "You know what I think?" she asked as she took two more steps toward the front of the ship. "I think it's going to be a long trip."

The Treelanders had sailed past the stone arch into the forbidden land for the first time in their lives. The tall ship began to pick up speed. It charged smoothly through the waves into the huge, choppy sea. Avry was at the wheel of the ship, although it was nothing like the small boat that he sailed at Sky Lake with his dad. Every weekend the boys went fishing with their dad, and Avry would always get a chance to sail the boat. His dad would always shout, "Captain Avry! Captain Avry's at the wheel!" Now his happy thoughts quickly disappeared, however. His dad was not there, and Avry felt a great emptiness in his heart.

An hour had passed since the Treelanders had left their village. The tired sun submerged beneath the horizon, revealing the thirteen moons of Epalushia: twelve small moons that orbited a large one. Trueman sat close to Avry and helped him navigate the ship, while Caitlyn cooked the fish that Emelia and Willow had caught.

"When do you think we'll see Raider?" Trueman asked.

"Don't know. Zita told me this ship would catch up to him fast, but I don't see a thing in any direction," Avry replied.

"You guys, it's time to eat!" Caitlyn called from the ship's cabin.

Avry refused to eat; he had much preferred to stay on deck and keep and eye out for Raider. His siblings, on the other hand, were starving, and went below for dinner. The sky was full of stars that sparkled like fireflies on a hot summer night in Treeland, and the thirteen moons provided enough light for Avry to keep watch for the evil sea monkey. His frustration escalated as he steered the ship from left to right, the sea still and empty. He even tried looking through his looking glass, but the world was unfocused. Avry suddenly remembered the map that the knight had given him back at the lake and took it from his backpack. The yellowish brown parchment was very old and rolled up with a small, red string. He unrolled the map and could not believe his eyes—the map was completely black.

"A lot of good this is going to do me," he said to himself.

He turned over the map to see if there was anything on the other side, but as far as he could see it was just a piece of old rotten paper.

"Okay, let's see...It's called a starlight map, and

the stars are shining bright...and..."

"Yaw not doin' it right," squawked a voice directly behind Avry.

Avry was so startled by the voice that the hair on his arms stood straight up. He quickly pulled out his sword and whipped around to see what had snuck up on him.

When Avry turned around he found the strangest-looking bird sitting on a barrel holding a crystal flower in his beak. The bird's feathers were yellowish blue and tattered; he had a small eye patch over his left eye and wore a pair of blue pants with straps that swung over his shoulders to keep them from falling down. The bird gently put down the flower, made a loud squawking sound, and then cleared his throat.

"Spikey Bluejeans at yaw service," the bird squawked.

"Are you a pirate? Wait a minute, what am I saying?...you're a talking b..."

"Parrot...not pirate, young man. I once waahs a parrot of a pirate, but not anymore."

"So how did you get here, and what do you know about this map?" Avry said curiously.

"Zita sent me to give yaw a little help and guidance with this here map. This map, as yaw must know, has three uses—two that I know of and one that my old master wouldn't share with me, or anyone else, for that matter."

"Who was your old master?" Avry asked.

"Raider was of course, well until Zita saved me, that is. You see Raider was once a dragon slayer and he got in a heavy fight with Zita. Zita won the fight, and Raider fled off and left me behind with nowhere to live."

Avry flapped the map in the bird's face, demanding, "So now tell me about this map."

"First thing you've gawt to do is roll the map up, the way it was given to you at the lake," Spikey squawked, and continued. "Now...the first use of the map is to look through it, like a looking glass. You will be able see things that you can't normally see. Secondly, look up to the stars and you can see a map of where you have traveled so you don't get lost. And I'm not really sure how the third and most important piece of this map works, but I do know that yaaaw can look at this map, and somehow it will show yaw a detailed map of Epalushia."

Avry quickly rolled the map back up, placed it up to his right eye, and looked into the tube to view the dark and empty ocean. Suddenly a beam of light shot out into the distance from the end of the tube, revealing objects he hadn't seen just seconds before.

"Whaaat da yaw see?" Spikey asked knowingly.

"Wow! I can't see Raider, but I can see some land ahead with a tall mountain and a cave."

Avry looked in all directions through the tube, but there was still no sign of Raider's ship. The rest of the Treelanders had finished their dinner and came up on the ship's deck to find out why Avry was talking to himself.

Emelia was still stuffing her face with wild cocoa berries as she slowly walked up to Avry and Spikey.

"Where did you get that scruffy old thing?"

Emelia pointed at the bird.

Avry smiled and announced to his crew, "Everyone, this is Spikey Bluejeans. Zita sent him here to help us find Raider."

"How is a bird gonna help us?" Willow bickered. "He's cute, but...really."

"Spikey is my name, please stop cawlling me bird, and don't cawll me cute!"

Spikey flew over to Avry and sat on his shoulder.

Everyone gathered around Avry in a circle and introduced themselves to Spikey. They all sat back and listened quietly as Spikey told them his amazing adventures with Raider. The night had become quiet, the water was smooth like glass, and it appeared that they would not catch up to the evil sea monkey and capture the egg that night.

Chapter 4
A Pirate's Twist

The Treelanders were fascinated while they listened to Spikey's amazing stories. Willow however was distracted when she caught sight of the crystal flower. She walked over nonchalantly and picked it up. "What's this?" Willow asked. She gazed into its sparkling beauty. "It's wonderful, can I have it?"

"That flower you hold has magical powers that will help yaaaw get the dragon egg back from Raider," Spikey said.

"Oh yeah, what kind of powers?" asked Trueman.

"I'm not sure exactly, but Zita specifically told me to aim the crystal at the egg and say this short phrase: *Warps of Zephyr.*"

"Well, that's great, except we can't find Raider," Caitlyn complained.

"Yaw gotta use the map for that," squawked Spikey.

"Avry, take out the map, look up to the stars, and then tell us what yaw see."

Avry looked again into the tube, but this time he aimed it straight up into the sky. Shooting stars began to cascade and swirl like a kaleidoscope until they formed into familiar objects in the sky.

"I can see our home, and Jewlz, the dragon...there's the la...hey! I can see our ship! Wait a minute...this map must not be working right."

"Why? What do you see, Avry?" Trueman asked.

"Well, there's a small object behind us and two large objects that just appeared on each side of us."

Everyone looked around eagerly, but there was nothing to be seen in any direction. Willow began to climb the rope ladder that went to the lookout tower. She looked in every direction for Raider's ship, and a sudden strong breeze blew her backward and threatened to knock her off.

Swirling dark clouds began to fill the sky, colorful flashes of lightning shot down into the water, and rolling thunder shook the ship like an earthquake. Strong winds filled the ship's big, red sails and pushed the ship faster through the choppy water. The waves grew higher and splashed down hard on the ship's deck, tossing and turning everyone on board.

A high wall of water bubbled around the ship until finally two fountains shot up into the air from both sides of the vessel.

Willow looked down into the water and screamed. "There's something under us—something really big!"

Bang! Boom!

Two cannonballs shot out of the water from both sides of the ship and flew into the air.

"What is it, Willow?" Caitlyn asked in a panic.

But before Willow could answer, the tops of two sails arose from the mysterious ocean. Cannonballs filled the air rapidly with fire and puffs of black smoke. The smoke was so rich that it burned their nostrils. They could taste the gunpowder as they inhaled. And as they tried to catch their breath, two large pirate ships appeared through the billowing cloud of death.

The brown ship on their right had ten angry-looking pirates, and the captain of the ship was all dressed in purple and black. A golden sash hung from his waist; and he was clearly the nastiest pirate on the ship. His face was gray and rough with a large, black beard that hung from his protruding chin. He wore two black, metal gloves, and in one he clenched tightly onto his long shiny sword. The captain raised his weapon high in the air and screamed to his mates, "Hold yer fire, mates!"

He looked fiercely into the eyes of his enemy, pointed his sword, and yelled, "Raider, hand over that treasure!"

The Treelanders couldn't believe their eyes when they looked to the ship where the captain had pointed. Five sea monkeys dressed like pirates were crouched down behind crates and barrels on the large, green ship to their left. And then a sea monkey with a small patch of orange, spiked hair arose from behind a rusted steering wheel. He stood up, brushed some seaweed off his shoulder, and then snarled, exposing his slimy green teeth.

It was Raider, and directly behind him, tied to a crate, was the beautiful shining dragon egg for everyone to see.

"You'll have to fight me for my treasures, Captain Slaughter!"

"Then prepare for your ship to be turned to dust," the captain replied.

The Treelanders were too stunned and frightened to move, not knowing what the pirates were up to.

"See kids, I told yaw that map would help us find Raider," squawked Spikey.

"Maybe we should just hide and act like we're not here," Trueman whispered.

"We're getting that egg if it's the last thing we do," Willow snapped.

For only a moment Raider and Captain Slaughter sneered silently into each other's eyes. Finally, Captain Slaughter raised his black, steel fist high in the air and called to his crew, "Fire!"

Sea monkeys swung over to Slaughter's ship on ropes that hung from the ship's enormous white sails. Cannonfire battered down relentlessly on Raider's ship. Pirates and sea monkeys clashed swords, while the two ships exchanged cannonfire. Black smoke clouded the air again, and the Treelanders were right in the middle of an all-out pirate fight.

Raider quickly untied the egg and rolled it toward the back of his ship. Captain Slaughter bounced from the Treelanders' ship over to Raider's ship and then let out an evil laugh as his sword struck a sea monkey in passing. "Argh, that treasure's all mine!" he shouted.

The Treelanders stood and watched as Captain Slaughter met Raider face to face. The two pirates snarled at each other, gripping their swords, and then engaged in a heavy battle, clashing and slashing.

"We've gotta do something," Emelia cried out.

Just then a loud *crackle* and *bang* erupted from the front of the Treelander's ship. A large pirate and an old-looking sea monkey had fallen onto their ship and were wrestling on the front deck. Then another small pirate with tight clothes and a big belly tossed a big, fat, green sea monkey onto their ship. He crashed through the floor and left a huge hole the size of a gorilla in the deck.

"That does it!" Avry yelled. His face was scarlet, and he scowled, "Emelia and Willow, you get the egg. Caitlyn, you come with me, and Trueman, you stay here and watch over Spikey and the ship."

"How come I always miss out on all the fun?" Trueman whined.

"Just stay here and don't do anything stupid," Avry said.

Willow grabbed the crystal flower and went to the edge of the ship with Emelia to retrieve the egg, while Avry and Caitlyn raced to the front of their ship. Avry began fighting with a pirate, and Caitlyn clashed with a sea monkey.

A loud crash echoed from Raider's ship, and pieces of wood and debris cluttered the sky. The evil sea monkey's ship was on fire and began sinking into the ocean, while Raider and Slaughter remained on board in a heavy battle. The dragon egg rolled down the ship's deck as it tilted backward and sank further into the water.

More pirates and sea monkeys had come aboard the Treelanders' ship and continued to battle, while Trueman and Spikey hid inside a barrel, watching everything though a small hole on the side.

"We can't just hide in here all day, Spikey. We've got to help," Trueman grumbled.

"Be patient, and watch," squawked Spikey.

Trueman peered out across the ship. He watched Emelia struggling to keep a pirate from knocking her overboard, while Willow aimed the crystal flower at the rolling dragon egg. The egg took one bounce off a wooden crate and flew into the air. Willow's hand trembled while trying to keep the crystal flower pointed steadily at her target.

Something else caught Trueman's eye. Captain Slaughter tossed Raider overboard and dashed after the egg that hung in the air, almost in a slow-motion flight. Finally, the youngest Treelander stood up in the barrel and yelled to Willow, "Say the darn spell already!"

A tall, brawny pirate gave Trueman an evil stare. He quickly pushed his enemy sea monkey toward the barrel containing Trueman and Spikey and knocked it over onto its side. The barrel wobbled and rolled toward the edge of the ship.

Just as Willow shouted the spell—"Warps of Zephyr"—Trueman, Spikey, and the barrel came crashing into her. She dangled helplessly over the side of the ship and screamed for Emelia. Sparks erupted out of the end of the crystal flower, and a bolt of lightning exploded into the water, missing the egg completely. The ocean turned and twisted, faster and faster, until a huge whirlpool formed next to the Treelanders' ship.

The madness went deadly silent for a moment; everyone stopped short and watched helplessly while the dragon egg was pulled toward the whirlpool's mouth. It was utter silence and bitter panic. Then, in a blink of an eye, the fighting resumed and the race for the precious dragon egg began.

Emelia clutched onto Willow's legs and helped her back onto the ship, while Willow screamed hysterically about something that Emelia couldn't comprehend.

"Look Emelia..." Willow blabbered, "...there's that guy again behind us—and he's on a raft." She stood back on the ship and pointed behind her. Emelia looked back but there was no one there. She rubbed her round-tipped nose with the palm of her hand and squinted. "Willow, you must have bumped your head hard, because there is nobody out there. Now let's get that egg before it's too late."

On the opposite side of the whirlpool, Captain Slaughter stomped his feet like a little baby, and said, "I must have that golden egg!" He sprung toward the egg, while Raider's ship continued to crumble and twist into tiny bits and pieces. Fractured splinters of wood exploded into the air and rained into the ocean. What had once been the sea monkey's noble ship now littered the water that surrounded them. Slaughter scowled when he saw Willow's rescue attempt right in front of his evil eyes.

Willow hung on a beam from one of the ship's sails, while Emelia swung her out over the water. Willow's large feet clutched the beam; she hung upside down, and she stretched to reach the escaping egg. Beads of sweat rolled into her eyes and burned like fire. She blindly lunged forward and snatched the egg. She held it tight while Emelia pulled her back toward the ship. The girls smiled in triumph as they held the beautiful egg in their hands. And then—

Captain Slaughter grabbed Willow along with the egg. He kicked Emelia in the stomach; she doubled over, and threw up onto the deck. Then the captain swung toward his mighty ship on a knotted rope.

"Let me go!" Willow howled. She kicked, then spat, "You want this...?" She held up the sparkling egg in front of Slaughter's ragged face. Then, without warning, she let go of the egg. The precious treasure dropped onto the Treelanders' ship. The egg's fall was softened when it crashed on top of two pirates and knocked them out cold. "...then go fetch it!" Willow shouted.

"You pesky little pain, you will pay for this!" Captain Slaughter shouted.

Trueman and the pirates scuffled to get the egg as it spun like a top toward the edge of the ship. A huge pirate with a shiny, bald head snatched the egg in the crook of his arm and ran for Slaughter's ship. He snarled and panted at Trueman, while he charged toward him. "Outta me way, ya little scruff," he grunted.

Spikey grabbed the end of a rope that was tied to an anchor and flew it over to Trueman. "Yaw know what they say..." Spikey snickered, "...the bigger they are, the harder they *FALL!*"

Boom! Splash!

Trueman and Spikey held tight to the rope that tripped the pirate overboard and sent the egg back up into the air. The dragon egg bounced off one of the ship's sails and sprung over to Slaughter's ship.

"Avry, help me!" Willow cried, struggling relentlessly to get free from Captain Slaughter.

Avry's heart pounded in his ribcage. His sister's cry made his hair stand on end. He watched Willow struggle in the captain's greasy clutches, and he gritted his teeth. "Hold on, Willow!" he howled as he jumped onto Slaughter's ship. Avry's head began to spin when he turned and saw the rest of the Treelanders deep in battle. His brother and sisters were trying to fight off the other pirates that surrounded them from all sides. There was chaos all around, and Avry felt his stomach churn and harden.

Captain Slaughter held Willow tight in one arm, while he gripped his sword in the opposite hand. He barred his lips to a thin white line and then chomped his crooked teeth. The pirate spat at Avry and held his foot firm on top of the egg.

"What ya gonna do boy?" the captain said in a scruffy voice.

"Let her go, Slaughter!" cried Avry. He pulled his sword out and charged at Slaughter.

"Yer gonna have ta kill me for that," the captain laughed.

If there ever was a beginning of a hero's life, this was it for Avry. He and Captain Slaughter's swords connected with great force. Sparks rained into the air as the swords clashed. It remains a wonder why the vibration didn't crack the egg open. The Treelander had never fought a pirate before, but he had been trained by Prince William, one of the best swordsmen in Epalushia, and he fought without fear. His sword crashed down on Slaughter's shoulder, startling the pirate. Slaughter looked stunned as he clutched his bloody shoulder. While he was distracted in pain, Willow kicked him in the leg, and the egg rolled back into the water.

Captain Slaughter's heart jumped to his throat when Raider popped out of the water, laughed wildly, captured the precious egg once again, and dove into the whirlpool.

"Now look what you've done, missy, you've lost my treasure!" Slaughter fumed. He shoved Willow inside the ship's cabin, slammed the door shut, and clicked the lock.

Avry's head spun in circles. First his sister had been captured, and now he heard more screams—screams of terror from the Treelanders' ship. The pirates had captured Caitlyn, Trueman, Spikey, and Emelia, and then walked them to a wooden plank that hung from the ship's side. Avry heard Slaughter laugh wickedly from behind him. "It doesn't get better than this, me lad."

Avry brushed off the comment and watched as a huge, bald pirate pointed his sword at his siblings, backed them closer to the end of the plank, and commanded, "This is our ship now, kids. Ye best be walking the plank." The pirate poked his sword at the Treelanders until, one by one, the kids fell into the raging water below. Spikey swooped into the air and raced off to help Avry. Trueman, Emelia, and Caitlyn watched Avry as he stood face to face with Captain Slaughter; they struggled to get free from the whirlpool that sucked them closer, inch by inch, second by second. They barely heard Willow's scream, but they looked up helplessly.

Willow pounded from inside Slaughter's ship, but it was no use; the captain had locked the door shut and pocketed the key.

"Let her out!" Avry cried. He swung his sword, just missing Slaughter's face. There was a whoosh of air that passed by the pirate's ear, and he chuckled and burped. "Young lad, now it's your turn to learn a lesson. Never mess with Captain Slaughter!"

He raised his arm and took one swing at Avry's sword, slicing it into two pieces. Avry was left without a weapon and moved closer to the side of the ship.

Avry felt blackness closing in around his eyes. He reached for his sword, but it wasn't there. It was a vision that he had seen before. The dream-demon had him trapped in its web again. He felt a lump in his throat and couldn't breathe. But he wasn't sleeping. This was real, and this was no time for passing out. He shook his head clear from the spiders of fear and snapped to it when he heard screams from below.

"Avry, help!" Caitlyn hollered as she spiraled into the whirlpool. She held hands with Trueman and Emelia, and then, in a blink of an eye, they were gone.

"Nooooooooooo!" Avry screamed. His heart

raced as he stood, watching.

"Now don't you worry, you are about to meet up with them in a minute," Slaughter said, with no remorse.

"What about my sister? Let her go. She's no use to you," he replied, fighting to hold back tears.

"Very touching, my son," the captain said and then pushed Avry closer to the edge of the ship. "I'll make a deal with ye. Bring back my treasure and ye can have ye precious sister back. Now swim like a good little Treelander."

Captain Slaughter pushed Avry backward. Avry reached out and grabbed Captain Slaughter's hand as he slipped toward the water. The cold black metal glove slipped off, exposing the captain's mutilated skin. Slaughter winced at the unbearable pain, and he held his decrepit hand as he turned away and entered his ship. The rest of his crew quickly boarded the ship and joined the captain inside.

Avry splashed into the water and grabbed onto a wooden plank. He flapped his arms like a bird and tried desperately to get away from the clutches of the swirling mass of water.

The water around Captain Slaughter's ship bubbled and hissed. Then the huge ship submerged under the water and was quickly out of sight.

Spikey appeared from nowhere and dodged over to help Avry escape from the mighty tug of the whirlpool.

"Spikey, go get Zita!" Avry tried to catch his breath, as the water reached his lips. "Tell him we need his h..." he gurgled.

Avry stretched his hands into the sky, and Spikey tried to pull him out, but the current was too strong for the little old parrot.

Spikey watched helplessly while his friend vanished into the whirlpool. He was left alone to travel back for help. As he flew higher in the sky, he looked back only once to see what made a loud, wood- splitting sound. He was amazed to see the back end of the Treelanders' ship had been pulled into the hungry mouth of the gigantic whirlpool. It only took seconds, and then everyone and everything had vanished. No more battling pirates, no more sea monkeys, and most unfortunate of all—no more Treelanders.

Chapter 5
Vortex to Vorack

Avry tried desperately to hold his breath as the dark black vortex pulled him deeper into the unknown. Flashes of sparkling lights passed in front of his eyes, forming a circle around the dark core of the whirlpool. Avry's skin felt like it had been pelted with millions of pins and needles as he sped faster and deeper into the pit. The water current twisted Avry's helpless body, as if it had a craving to pull him apart. His ears popped and cracked from the loud pulsing sound that pressed against his head. As each second passed, Avry waited for a chance to catch his breath, but it felt like that moment would never come, until finally his body catapulted up and out of the water.

Avry's body was sprawled out over a bed of rocks. Sounds of steam hissed and puffed throughout the room as he rested, half-unconscious, and tried to regain his strength. He slowly opened his eyes and took a deep breath when he saw the colorful reflections and shimmering lights from the crystal-formed stalagmites that grew in the bed of the cave.

Voices from his brother and sisters bounced off the moist cave walls that dripped with beads of water. Avry opened his eyes wider to focus on the figure running toward him.

"Trueman, is that you?" Avry asked wearily and rubbed his eyes.

There was a soft rumble that shook the cave floor, sending small pieces of rock and dust flying into the air while Trueman, Caitlyn, and Emelia approached.

"Are you okay, Avry?" Trueman asked.

"Yeah, how bout you guys?"

"We're fine," said Trueman. "My head is still spinning a bit, though."

"Where's Willow and Spikey?" Emelia asked.

"I sent Spikey to get Zita and Zia, and Willow..." Avry's voice trailed off.

"Where is she, Avry?" Caitlyn asked boldly.

"Well, the only way we are going see her again is if we get that egg back," Avry said, trying desperately to hold back tears. "It was Captain Slaughter, he kidnapped Willow on his ship, and there was nothing I could do to save her without the dragon egg."

"It's okay, Avry, we'll get her back," Trueman said, putting his arms around his brother.

They paused for a moment when the temperature suddenly turned extremely hot, the cave began to shake again, and white, sizzling steam blasted up from cracks in the floor.

"Let's get outta here before I combust," Emelia said.

The Treelanders started to walk down a small path in the cave and around a small pool of water where the whirlpool had carried them. The hot steam on the water quickly evaporated and froze solid from the frigid cold air that pushed its way through the cave.

“For a place so beautiful, I don’t like this constant climate change,” Emelia complained.

“It’s not just the temperature that’s changing, look!” Trueman exclaimed, pointing toward the wall in front of them. The wall had turned from dark, solid rock into a clear wall of water that shook like a blob of jelly. Caitlyn walked cautiously toward the wall and reached her hand out to the blob of water.

“Don’t touch it!” cried Emelia, “Maybe it’s catchy!”

They all were fascinated as they watched Caitlyn’s arm disappear straight through the wall into the water blob.

“Wow, this is cool,” Caitlyn said. “It’s starting to get cold though, and tighter...” She snapped her hand out just before the wall turned back to solid rock. “Yikes!”

“Come on, we really need to get outta here right now,” Avry said.

“Look, footprints. These look like they must be Raiders’,” Trueman concluded.

The siblings followed the footprints for a while as the temperature continued to change from hot to cold and the ground shook every so often. The Treelanders stopped dead in their tracks when they heard a scream that came from a dark tunnel to their left. Avry quickly grabbed the starlight map, put it up to his eye, and looked into the dark tunnel. A beam of light shot down the tunnel and made it possible for Avry to see.

“It’s a girl,” said Avry. “She looks like she’s stuck in some sort of hole.”

The Treelanders climbed into the tunnel and sank up to their waists in water except for Trueman who was trying to keep his head from getting wet. The scream from the girl grew louder, and the Treelanders trudged forward into the dark and gloomy tunnel.

"Hello there!" Caitlyn yelled to the girl.

"Hold on, little girl!" Trueman shouted.

"Trueman...I never said she was little," Avry said, smirking at his brother.

The girl didn't answer; she just screamed and yelled about something, something that the Treelanders couldn't understand.

"Yaowao...shounomono...noraaaaack!"

"Sounds like a burlybeast running from Trueman," Avry said, jokingly.

"Hey!" Trueman cried. "They didn't...I mean, it wasn't my fau—"

"Enough, you two," Caitlyn said with a scowl.

The tunnel was dimly lit from something far ahead of them. Water dripped on their heads continuously while they searched for the girl.

The Treelanders finally reached a large, brightly lit cave at the end of the tunnel. The walls were covered with beautiful, shiny, colored rocks that glittered from a glowing object in the room.

"Look, there she is!" Trueman shouted, pointing at the girl.

The Treelanders ran quickly to the girl who struggled in a large, green, slime-like pit. The girl was buried up to her shoulders; her long blonde hair and creamy white face glowed with colors coming from the object that she held tight in her hands over her head.

"Hold on, we'll get you out," Avry said and then climbed near the edge of the slime pit. "Okay guys, I'll hold on to her, and you guys pull us back out." He carefully leaned over and grabbed the girl under her arms while Caitlyn, Emelia, and Trueman formed a chain and held him in place.

"Please don't let the Vorack fall," the girl shouted as they began to pull her out.

"There she goes again, talking all weird," Trueman said.

"Pull!" Avry cried. "Pull!" His face scrunched and contorted.

The slime around the girl started to pop when they pulled her from the pit. The slime crept slowly up the girl's body and onto Avry's hands. They struggled to break her free from the growing slime.

"Hurry up! This thing is trying to eat us, I think!" Avry cried, slime- covered up to his elbows.

The gurgling slime pulled them closer and closer toward the pit. Green oozing goop had completely covered Avry and reached onto Caitlyn and Emelia's hands.

The object in the girl's hands twisted and turned into different shapes. An array of colorful light fanned out of the sphere and painted the cave walls.

Trueman struggled to reach for something in his backpack while he continued to hold onto Caitlyn's arm.

Suddenly a high-pitched sound filled and enraptured the room.

Toot!

Weeee!

Toot!

Caitlyn barely managed to stretch her neck around to get a glimpse of the music maker. From the corner of her eye she witnessed the most amusing sight. Trueman held his wooded flute between his puckered lips and puffed a happy tune. His olive-green face was now a shade of crimson, and he tooted the wooden instrument with a relaxed and joyful smile.

The slime relaxed on their skin and began to retreat and slither back into the pit.

"It's working!" cried Caitlyn. "Keep playing, Trueman!"

Toot!

Tweet!

Weee!

Trueman continued to play until the slime had completely released everyone from its slimy grip.

"It's off us...pull, quick!" Avry shouted.

They all tugged and pulled the girl safely to the edge of the pit and then stared at her, bewildered.

The girl was wearing a dress made of blue-colored seashells that covered her entire body down to a fish-like fin where normally her feet should have been.

"You're a mermaid, aren't you?" Trueman asked with his mouth dropped wide open.

"Yes I am. My name is Alexia," the girl said with a smile.

"Trueman, how did you know to play your flute?" Caitlyn asked.

"I read a story from the Tree of Life one night about Grandpa Johnny. He told a tale about when he fell in one of these slime pits and he sang his way out."

"Thank you, little boy; your smart thinking saved me and the Vorack," Alexia said.

"The name is Trueman. These are my sisters, Caitlyn and Emelia, and this is my brother, Avry."

"It's very nice to meet you all," Alexia smiled. "Welcome to my world."

"So how did you get stuck down here?" Emelia asked.

"These are the great coral caves that are usually filled with water. I was searching for Vorack and suddenly the water disappeared," Alexia said.

"What is a Vorack?" Emelia said, puzzled.

Alexia held out the bright shiny orb in front of her. It continued to change shapes and colors as it sat in her hands. "This is Vorack, the spirit of the ocean, the protector of the vortex and the great coral mountain."

"How did Vorack get here?" Avry asked.

"Something forced the vortex open and pushed Vorack down into the caves. Soon my people will perish if I don't get Vorack to the top of the mountain and close the vortex."

"I don't think we understand, where are your people and why will they perish?" Caitlyn asked as she looked around the cave.

"The caves are empty, the coral mountain has

begun to freeze, hot springs are erupting in the caves, and without the vortex covered it has caused a great disturbance in our life force," said Alexia, and then looked to her fin that slowly transformed into feet.

"We'll help you, won't we, guys?" Trueman looked to his brother and sisters.

"Sure we'll help, but you need to help us find our way out of here to catch up with a sea monkey named Raider," Avry said.

The mermaid nodded, "My people and I know of the evil Raider. We will show you the cave that he traveled out. Come with me. We must hurry."

Alexia guided the Treelanders through caves that shook with tremors and boiled with hot springs until they finally came to the biggest cave of them all. There were pools of water with mermaids and mermen all through the huge cave. A large merman, holding a wooden spear, ran over to Alexia the minute she entered the cave, and exclaimed, "Alexia, you found Vorack!"

"Yes, Father, and these people are here to help us return it to the top of the mountain."

"I am Pertaka. Welcome to the grand coral cave," Alexia's father said.

Alexia told the merpeople what happened to her and how she found Vorack with the help of the Treelanders.

"Come and join us. You must feast and then rest before you climb the great Coral Mountain," Pertaka said as he held out a hand to a pathway made of blue shells and red starfish. At the end of the path they found a small village of merpeople. The merpeople hurried about, preparing for a grand feast. In a very short while there was a parade with streamers, music, cheering, and most of all...the Treelanders were the honored guests.

At the feast, the Treelanders enjoyed the buffet of many unusual things to eat. Avry told their story to the merpeople—about Raider, Captain Slaughter, Willow getting captured, and the dragon egg— while the rest of the kids enjoyed wild squid-didos.

Emelia was in heaven when they finally served dessert, which included coral candy, cinnamon star sticks, gummy seaweed, and chocolate-covered snails.

After the feast, Alexia showed the Treelanders to a small, dry room with four stone beds covered in sea sponges and a bright, warm fireplace in the corner that lit the room.

"Rest while you can. It's a long way up the mountain to return Vorack to where he belongs," Alexia said while leaving the room.

"Thanks, I don't think we'll have any problems resting," Avry said nodding toward Trueman, Caitlyn, and Emelia who were already lying in bed.

"Wow, Avry, I can't believe we had dinner with mermaids," Trueman said.

"Yeah, the food wasn't bad either."

Just then Caitlyn began to cry and sat upright in bed.

"What's wrong, Caitlyn?" Emelia asked. "Are you homesick? Didn't you like the food?"

"We were supposed to be eating at King Oliver's

castle. I was looking forward to a dance with Prince William. And look at me—I'm a mess!" Caitlyn cried hysterically.

"I think all of us just need some sleep. You'll feel better in the morning, Caitlyn," Avry said, as reflections from the fireplace danced on his face.

Emelia sang everyone to sleep with one of their mother's favorite songs that she sang to comfort the children on many restless nights.

Chapter 6
Coral Mountain

Far under the ocean and miles away from the Coral Mountain, a different kind of chaos was brewing on board Captain Slaughter's ship. Willow was driving her own sort of ship, and it was called *chaos*. She barked feverously at a big, bald pirate named Slug from inside her jail cell. She scooped the pirate-made stew from a bowl and chucked it at Slug. "You call this food?!" she hollered, and then spat phlegm on the bald pirate's nose. "I've eaten dirt that tasted better!" she shouted, smashing the bowl on the floor into bits.

"I don't think she likes ye cooking, Slug," said a short pirate named Willy. He laughed and coughed heartily while Slug wiped his face clean.

"It's toilet slop!" Willow said as her voice cracked. "How about some real food, you filthy rotten pirate?!"

"She's a feisty one, eh, Slug?" Willy said, as he picked his grimy teeth.

"When I get outta here, you're gonna be the one that walks the plank!" Willow shouted, and spat more phlegm at Willy.

The door barged open, and Captain Slaughter entered the room with an evil smirk stretching from ear to ear. "Forget the girl for now, boys. Raider has been spotted on the scope, and we're bringing the ship up. All hands on deck!" he shouted.

While Captain Slaughter and his crew were busy

getting their ship ready to chase after Raider, the Treelanders were sound asleep back at the coral caves. Suddenly a loud explosion shook the cave, and toppled everyone to the floor.

Alexia ran into the room with a panicked look on her face and tried to talk while catching her breath. "Raider was here...he blocked the cave...that leads to the top of the mountain."

"Did he have the dragon egg with him?" Trueman asked.

"Yes," Alexia replied. "One of our guards saw him running with a large, sparkling object."

"Well, how are we going to get to the top of the mountain now?" Avry asked grimly.

"Let's go see my father. He'll know," Alexia said.

The Treelanders grabbed their belongings and went out into the grand cave where Pertaka was talking to other mermen. He approached the Treelanders as they walked toward him, "There is only one other way for you to get to the top of Coral Mountain. You will need to go through the caves that are still flowing with water. These caves will only take you halfway up the mountain and lead you to a trail that you can follow up to the top."

Caitlyn looked bothered and said, "How are we going to get through the water? We are not merpeople like you."

Pertaka reached into a funnel-shaped spongy rock, and held out what looked like mica-covered shells and said, "Take these breathing shells and hold them over your nose and mouth. You will have enough air to breathe until you get to the outside path." He handed each Treelander a shell that, up close, looked like an oversized snail.

Alexia pulled Vorack out of a pouch that she wore and gave it to Trueman. Vorack's bright light and colors vanished as a hard, gray layer formed around the small orb.

Trueman took Vorack, put him in his backpack, and held it tight to his waist. He smiled fondly and said, "Don't worry, Alexia, we'll get him back were he belongs." His cheeks flushed.

She rubbed Trueman's cheek with her soft hand, saying, "When you get to the very top of the mountain, you will find a small hole. You must place Vorack in the hole, and he will bring balance back to our life force. Then the ocean will rise again and cover the coral mountain."

Alexia, Pertaka, and several other merpeople led the Treelanders to a small cave opening on the far side of the grand cave. The ground shook, hot steam erupted through cracks in the cave floor, and pieces of rocks fell onto everyone. The swooshing sound of raging water filled the black cave hole as they neared the opening.

"Good luck, and go in peace," Alexia said, giving each Treelander a hug before they climbed into the hole.

Avry was the last one to climb into the hole. He poked his head back out after he saw the water rushing through the cave like a huge waterfall. He asked, "How are we going to swim up through these caves? The water will just push us back down!"

"Swim straight down with the current and then

toward the center of the mountain," Pertaka said. "Once the water current subsides, begin to proceed upward through the purple crystal caves."

Avry shook his head and jumped down into the hole with the others. *Purple crystal caves. Purple crystal caves.* He repeated this over and over in his head. "Okay guys, hold tight to each other, and follow me," he said, and then put the breathing shell up to his face.

Avry, panic stricken, looked at his brother and sisters, and jumped into the wild river that roared into the bowels of the cave. Trueman, Caitlyn, and Emelia followed behind Avry. The water pushed them down just like the whirlpool that had brought them here, except this time they were able to breathe while in the rush of water. The cold current pushed them further into the dark abyss until they hit the coral bottom. The raging water propelled them upward, further through the mountain's caves.

They moved through a dark, murky tunnel and headed toward the center of the mountain, just as Pertaka had instructed. Avry pulled out the starlight map, and the others followed the projected light. The push of the current had finally subsided, and the caves began to shimmer with colorful lights. The kids continued to push forward and swim further inward until they reached the purple crystal cave.

The cave grew bigger and brighter as they inclined up the mountain. Trueman held tightly to both Vorack and Caitlyn, while Emelia and Avry swam in front of them. Avry pointed to a bright light that beamed from above. Then more lights stunned them in their journey. There was a flash of red and yellow light, followed by an unexpected, huge explosion. The kids tumbled backward and rolled violently though the water, knocking Trueman's breathing shell out of his hands. Air bubbles rushed around their heads as Trueman scrambled to find his shell.

Bitter cold swept through the water current, and they struggled to regain focus on their direction toward the exit. Caitlyn and Emelia swam ahead, while Avry and Trueman shared a breathing shell. Within minutes after the explosion, a sudden breath of cold air hit their noses, and they found themselves in a small, clay-red cave.

Bombs blasted outside the cave entrance, while the Treelanders sat and caught their breath. A small cloud of smoke breezed passed them with a scent of sulfur and gunpowder.

"It's freezing up here," Emelia complained. She shivered in the cold breeze as it covered her wet skin.

Trueman clutched his waist, his hand fumbled awkwardly, and his eyes opened wide. He looked down and gulped when he noticed that his backpack with Vorack was no longer there. "Oh no!" he screamed, "the Vorack is gone! I must have dropped my pack during the blast." His body shook, and he felt his stomach turn inside out.

Avry gazed through the starlight map into the water-filled, purple, crystal cave. The beam of light fanned down the cave wall until it hit an unlikely sight. "There it is, hanging on a cliff!" he shouted, "it's not too far down."

"I'll go get it, Avry," Emelia said. "Trueman, stop worrying. You guys find out what's happening outside, and I'll catch up with you soon."

Avry, Caitlyn, and Trueman ran outside the cave entrance while thunderous blasts continued to explode from something above the mountaintop. Emelia wasted no time and jumped into the frigid-cold water. As she descended toward Trueman's backpack, she realized she didn't have the breathing shell with her and kicked faster. The backpack with the shiny orb inside was only a few feet below. She quickly grabbed the soggy brown backpack and swam back toward the surface. Her temples pounded as she held on to the last few seconds of oxygen.

Thump!

Her head hit a force field of clear rock consisting of a thick layer of ice that blocked her exit from the frigid pool of water. Bubbles escaped from her mouth while she panicked.

Outside, the others stood on the mountainside while snow fell heavily upon them. They couldn't believe their eyes when they looked up. Captain Slaughter's ship hovered over the mountain and blasted cannonballs toward Raider, who was trying desperately to climb up the mountain. Clutched firmly in Raider's green scaly hands, was, without a doubt, the precious diamond and gold decorated dragon egg.

"Captain Slaughter has Raider trapped. We should be able to catch up to him with no problem and get the egg," Trueman said.

Caitlyn tapped her index finger on her bottom lip, and said, "Maybe with all the distraction, one of us can sneak onto Slaughter's ship and get Willow."

"Why is Emelia taking so long?" Avry griped. "You guys go after Raider while I go get Emelia, and then we'll meet up with you."

Avry ran back into the cave, and his heart stopped. There was no sign of Emelia anywhere and, even more horrifying, a layer of ice covered the pool of water where they had arrived. Avry looked through the slab of ice and could see Emelia's blurry face below. She continued to struggle and scratch to get through the layer of ice, but it was hopeless. Avry found a large stick and pounded on the ice, while Emelia punched at it from below. The stick broke into pieces as the ice continued to grow thicker.

"Emelia...try using your sword!" Avry cried.

She watched Avry's distorted lips move up and down through the glass of ice; his voice was muffled and distant. Branches of ice began to form and creep onto Emelia's arms like snakes. They crackled like snapping twigs and continued to twist around her body. The eerie icicles pinched into her skin and burned like fire.

Suddenly blasts of warm light shot out from Trueman's backpack. Vorack let out a piercing sound and shattered the ice into pieces of slush. Avry immediately grabbed Emelia's hand and pulled her out of the icy sludge. She took a deep gasp for air that echoed throughout the cave and her lungs jumped for joy.

"Come on, let's catch up with the others," Avry

commanded. He pulled Emelia across the cave floor. Her frozen feet dragged, and she clutched Avry's shoulders. He took no notice of her stiff condition and pressed on.

Caitlyn and Trueman were already near the top of the mountain where Captain Slaughter's gunfire had Raider pinned into a corner. Raider cowered and covered the egg like a mother protecting her young. Raider looked behind him for an escape like a rat weaseled into a trap. *Pathetic* was the word that Caitlyn used to describe the monkey. She looked down and was relieved to see Emelia and Avry had made it back. Then she snapped her neck at the sound of a curdling scream.

Avry and Emelia looked up as well when they heard the scream from Slaughter's ship. They raced up the icy path that curved around the mountainside, carrying Trueman's backpack with the shiny orb inside.

"Avry...Emelia! Look up here!" shouted the familiar voice.

Avry and Emelia climbed higher up the path and found Trueman and Caitlyn sitting on a rock, breathing heavily.

"You guys, look, it's Willow!" Caitlyn cried as she panted and clutched her side.

Willow stuck her head out a small porthole on the side of Slaughter's ship and continued to scream. "Caitlyn, look behind you!" she shouted.

Caitlyn looked down the path and saw a dark figure ducking into a small cave, "Someone is following us, Avry," Caitlyn ranted.

“We don’t have time for that now,” Avry said, and then handed Trueman his frozen backpack. Vorack squirmed inside and began to hum.

Avry quickly devised a plan. “Trueman, head up to the top of the mountain and put Vorack where he belongs. Caitlyn and I will get the egg. Emelia, you go rescue Willow...oh, and Trueman..., I need your sword,” he smiled. He always made it sound so easy, but their adventure had just begun.

Trueman quickly tossed his sword to Avry and dashed up the mountainside. He snuck passed Captain Slaughter and Raider, who were busy clashing swords. As he reached the mountaintop, he looked down and watched Emelia struggle to get aboard Slaughter’s ship.

The wind was unbearable and made it nearly impossible for Emelia to grab a rope that dangled from the bottom of the vessel. A silver anchor hung on the rope and flailed in the breeze. Emelia’s feet slipped off the icy rock where she stood, and she floated outward toward the rope using her wings. She shimmied up the rope with lightning speed only to notice that Slug, the pirate, was climbing down toward her. Slug took out a large knife and began to cut the rope, while Emelia turned and scurried back down toward the anchor.

Snap!

Emelia fell in a downward spiral, her head missing collisions with several jutting rocks only by inches. Directly below her, she unexpectedly found Avry and Caitlyn. They crashed to the ground and sank into a bank of deep, fluffy snow.

"Well, that went well," Emelia said sarcastically and laughed. She licked the snow from her lips and smiled, while Avry and Caitlyn scowled back at her.

"Come on, let's get the egg," Avry said, jumping to his feet. He brushed himself off and looked upward at Trueman, who was climbing out of sight.

Trueman continued to watch Raider and Captain Slaughter fight senselessly over the egg, while the rest of the Treelanders approached from below. He shivered and could not move. He didn't want to go on alone, but he knew he had to. He looked below one last time and then proceeded on to the highest part of the mountain to return the orb to its home.

Back down on the mountainside, Caitlyn postured toward Raider. "Hand over the egg, Raider!" she shouted.

"Well, if it isn't another green worm," Captain Slaughter snickered.

"We're Treelanders, and that's our egg!" Avry said and stuck his chest out like a big man.

Raider became irritated and stomped his foot like a baby in a tantrum. "This fight is between Captain Slaughter and me! Neither you, nor any Treelander, including birdbrain Slaughter, will ever get this egg, if it's the last thing I do," he whined while he cradled the egg behind his back. He turned and kicked his large black boot into Captain Slaughter's stomach, sending the pirate crashing into the Treelanders, who fell like dominos down the mountainside, flopping like wet rags.

The egg thief climbed up the mountain and out of sight, while the others fought and struggled to climb back up. Slaughter's crew flew the pirate ship over toward a rock that jutted out from the mountainside where Captain Slaughter waited. Captain Slaughter quickly boarded his ship, with Willow still aboard, and sped off in pursuit of Raider. The Treelanders rushed up the mountainside to catch up with Trueman and watched Slaughter's ship zoom into the clouds.

Meanwhile, on top of the mountain, Trueman stood numb from the cold snow that pelted his body. He could see the puffs of his breath in the deathly cold air. His body stiffened, and his knees buckled. He crawled slowly to the small hole in the center of the mountaintop. It was only a few feet away, but yet they looked like miles. Out the corner of his eye, he watched Raider run past him, carrying the dragon egg. He paid no attention and continued to crawl forward. The orb began to pulse more with each step closer to its happy abode. Trueman pushed away a pile of snow and stretched his arms out over a small bottomless pit. "You're home, Vorack," he said with a frozen smile.

He dropped Vorack into the hole and watched the colorful lights explode upward from Vorack. The array of blinding light surrounded the entire mountain. The vortex was closed, the snow stopped, the ice melted and turned into rivers, and the raging streams rose over the mountaintop, filling the coral caves once again.

Before the youngest Treelander had a chance

to move, a strong vacuum of unsettling water pulled Trueman into the belly of the ocean, and he vanished.

Caitlyn, Emelia, and Avry floated side by side in the mysterious and unknown ocean. The egg was gone again; Willow was still a prisoner to Captain Slaughter, the tyrant; and they were far from home without their rightful belongings.

The sun was shining brightly with not a cloud in the sky. Neither wind nor rain brought on what the Treelanders encountered next. The water began to gurgle, and then water shot from beneath the settling waves, ripples turned to walls of water, and the rumble was sonic.

Fingers of water erupted around them, and they sat in the palm of a giant hand of rushing water. The wind was exuberant and the gale cried with a loud hiss. The enormous tidal wave carried the Treelanders miles and miles into the forbidden land. Their helpless bodies rode the hand of fury like dead fish being whipped through wild rapids.

Within just minutes, their soggy bodies landed on a small green sandy beach of a strange and uncharted island. They slept and dreamed that they were carried home. They hoped that when they opened their eyes, they would have the dragon egg, they would see their village in the pines, their family would be reunited, and the villagers would be cured from the gargoyle's fire and ice curse.

The dream was far from true, as shifty eyes watched the Treelanders while they slept on the beach. The bizarre green land was miles from home and filled with surprises. The journey to the giant's land, although purposeful, seemed endless.

Chapter 7
The Pot of Gold

The castaways from Treeland lay drained and exhausted from the wild water ride that carried them from Coral Mountain. Their bodies were scattered amongst the warm, green sandy beach, and the bright sun slowly baked them.

The only sounds were splashes of the soft ocean waves on the sandy green shore, and a woodpecker hammering the side of a large palm tree.

Avry popped his head up from the pile of sand where he had lain half-buried. The strong odor of salty fish made Avry sick to his stomach. He opened his mouth wide, gagged, and coughed up a large mouthful of green sand. "Plewth...yuck...where are we?" he said out loud. He looked left, then right, to get a response. There was no reply. He quickly realized he was alone and began to search along the shoreline for his siblings.

After a short while and with much relief, Avry found Caitlyn and Emelia, still passed out under a pile of sand and seaweed.

"Caitlyn, Emelia, wake up!" he said, while shaking them on the shoulders.

"Mmmm...this sand tastes like lime," Emelia said, as she sat upright.

"You have a serious taste bud problem, Emelia," Caitlyn said, and then pushed Emelia backward onto the sand.

"Avry, where's Trueman?" Emelia asked.

"I don't know, I don't see him anywhere," he replied.

Avry and Caitlyn walked up and down the beach looking for Trueman, while Emelia continued to eat the salty green sand. Their stomachs were in a knot as they worried about Trueman's whereabouts.

"Trueman!" they called.

"I hope he made it off the mountain," Avry said. His face looked ill, as his eyes peered out over the ocean.

"He must have, if we made it here...well, I'm sure..." Caitlyn said, panicked, and then chanted, "Trueman...Trueman...TRUEMAN!" She sounded like a wild tribe of headhunters; the only thing missing was the pounding of kettle drums.

"Up here!" Trueman shouted, "Up here!"

His feet kicked the air, while he hung from his backpack, which was snagged on a large palm tree branch.

"Get down here, and stop fooling around!" Avry snapped. "You had us worried to death." He stood with his arms crossed, tapping his right foot, his face scowling.

Trueman rocked himself back and forth to break free from the tree branch. "Look out, here I come...!" he yelled.

Crash!

Coconuts fell from the tree onto Avry and Caitlyn, and Trueman landed flat on his face in the sand.

"Are you done?" Avry barked. "We have to catch up to Raider and get that egg, or would you rather just sit around and play on the beach all day?" He turned and walked away from Trueman.

"But, Avry..." Trueman's voice trailed off, as he brushed sand off his chest.

"Somebody's in a bad mood," Caitlyn said. "Good to see you, Trueman, you had us worried, little brother."

"Thanks, Caitlyn," Trueman replied. "Where is Avry going, and why is Emelia eating the sand?"

"Don't even go there," Caitlyn moaned.

Avry was already on the other end of the beach, and the others hurried to catch up with him. "You guys, hurry up! Look!" he shouted. It appeared that his mood had quickly turned brighter.

Three figures stood near the woods in the distance, waving at the Treelanders while they approached.

"It's Zia and Zita!" Avry's happy voice shrilled. "And Spikey too!" he added.

Zia and Zita had funny smiles on their faces and waved continuously while Avry greeted them, "Wow! We are glad to see you— Okay, you guys can stop waving now."

"What's wrong with them?" Emelia asked, while she wiped green sand that glistened from her lips.

"They're in some sort of a trance," Trueman said, as he shook his head. "Maybe it was another gargoyle."

Caitlyn started to have a panic attack; she paced back and forth and breathed heavily. "Do something, Avry!" she screamed and pulled her hair. "Wake them up, we need help!"

Emelia slapped Caitlyn on the back of the head, and said, "Get a hold of yourself; we don't need you falling apart now!"

"I'm not falling apart," Caitlyn cried hysterically, rubbing the back of her head. "We're just in the middle of nowhere, our sister has been abducted by pirates, our parents have turned to statues of fire, we can't catch a stupid sea monkey that has an egg that Avry and Trueman never should have touched, and, on top of it all, my hair is a mess!"

"Here try some sand. It's really good," Emelia offered.

"Enough with your stupid SAND!" Caitlyn threw her hands into the air.

"Okay, I think the sun is really getting to us all," Avry said calmly.

Trueman approached Spikey and tried to shake him. Spikey, Zita, and Zia quickly vanished, and a small man in a green suit with a red beard, squinty eyes, and big round cheeks appeared in their place.

The little man took off his green top hat and bowed to greet them.

"Charlie McFarley at ya service. Welcome, hurry up, we must move quickly, or you'll be late to claim yer prize," said the jolly old leprechaun.

"What prize? We are looking for..." Trueman began to ask.

"Oh questions, yes, I see! How bout this one, to answer ye? You follow a rainbow to a land so bold, and ye find at the end a pot of gold," Charlie said in a singsong voice.

"Great, more gold," Emelia griped.

Avry looked at Charlie solemnly and said, "Look, mister, we are looking for a sea monkey named Raider, and he has the only treasure that we want."

"Oh I'm afraid that sore loser got tossed back," Charlie said with a slight chuckle.

"Sent back where?" Emelia asked.

"Over the rainbow, of course. And we sent that bad egg along with him. I must tell ye that the egg is no treasure. Ya see me brothers, Oscar and Degg, took the egg and put it in the field of gold treasures. The crazy monkey looked for hours to find his prize, and when he found it, the rainbow determined that the egg wasn't pure gold and diamonds."

"Well, it's worth more than gold where we come from," Caitlyn said proudly.

"What rainbow? How do we get to the rainbow?" Trueman asked.

Charlie paused for a minute and stared at them while he tugged at his beard, "Right then...enough talk. We must go now to collect your prize."

Charlie put his top hat on and tapped it twice; the bushes behind him disappeared, revealing a long green pathway. "Right this way, watch you step," he said as he held his hand out invitingly.

Long tree vines with four leaf clovers hung down on each side of the pathway. Only a thin strip of blue sky above lighted the thickly surrounded pathways. Celtic music filled the air, and a small leprechaun stepped out from the vines and started to play his bagpipes. The Treelanders were startled when they heard the sounds of a horse running behind them. Everyone except for Charlie turned to look for the horse, but there was nothing there except for steel horseshoes that left a trail on the green pathway in front of them.

"What is all this?" Emelia asked. "Am I dreaming?"

"Young girls and boys, this is the path of good luck," Charlie said, "but don't be easily fooled by its name. Remember, luck is only how you look at it, sometimes something bad could really be good luck."

Trueman shrugged his shoulder, looked at Avry, and then rolled his eyes back. "Avry, do you think this guy really knows what he's talking about? I mean he's kind of..."

BOOM!

The ground shook, the wind began to blow, and the tree vines began to wrap around the Treelanders' bodies like a snake coiling onto a tree branch.

"WEIRD!" a loud voice shouted.

"Let us go!" Caitlyn shrieked while she struggled to break herself free.

"Hey, where's Charlie? Where did he go?" Trueman asked.

"Wah Whoooo! You really do care about me!" cried Charlie.

Charlie reappeared under Trueman's feet and tickled him with a bright yellow feather.

"Why did you...think...I didn't care?" Trueman asked, giggling.

The tree vines released the Treelanders and dropped them onto the green pathway. Charlie McFarley stood in front of the Treelanders; he pulled at his beard and stared at his suit that changed into a bright yellow color.

"I can't believe me eyes! ME luck is changing kids."

Trueman gulped, "Sorry I called you weird."

"It's quite okay me friend. You see, I was growing very tired of that old green suit anyways. You should always be positive on the path of good luck; negative energy can really make a mess of things."

"How much longer will it be until we get to the rainbow, Charlie?" Emelia asked. "Are we even going to the rainbow?"

Charlie paused for a moment and stared at Emelia with a most- frozen smile. He said, "Right then...just this way to collect ye prize."

Charlie and the Treelanders traveled down the path until they came to an intersection with a path to the left and a path to the right. A leprechaun in a purple suit ran from the right path, pulled Emelia's hair, and laughed hysterically.

"Ouch! That's not funny!" Emelia griped.

"Oh don't mind Oscar. He's a real trickster," Charlie said, giggling.

"I'm sorry," Oscar groaned. "Here, try a delicious, sweet treat. I've got green sandbars, moonbeams, teardrops, toadstools, and golden chocolate."

The treats were mesmerizing. The enticing, sweet smells put Emelia into a trance. She licked her lips and reached out her hands.

"Oh yeah, I'll try them all!" Emelia shouted, as she grabbed a handful and tossed them in her mouth.

"No, no! You must only pick one!" Oscar hollered.

Emelia just kept chewing with joy at the delightful taste. "Mmmm mmm mmm," she said over and over.

"Oops…too late," Oscar said, as his eyes lit up.

Suddenly a leprechaun in a red suit ran out from the left path, kicked Caitlyn, and poked her in the eyes. And then he laughed so hard that he fell on his back and wiggled his legs in the air.

"Well, hello, Degg," Charlie snickered, "formal greetings as usual, aye boys."

"That's enough!" Avry snapped, anxious to be moving along. "Can we please stop all this fooling around and get to the rainbow? We are running out of time and we really need to catch Raider."

Charlie grinned and said, "Boys, these young folk aren't used to this kind of fun. Let's get them on their way to their prize." He tried hard not to laugh at Emelia, while she tugged at her lips.

"Mmmm…mmmmm…mmmm!" Emelia tried to talk, but she could not open her mouth.

"Ah yes, greed will kill the soul," said Oscar. "When you eat my sweets, don't take the whole lot; mixtures of these treats are sure to tie a knot," he sang like a nursery rhyme.

"Hey! Fix her lips you rotten…"

Before Avry could say another word, he sunk into a hole with only his head showing. Green sand spun around his struggling head.

"Okay, okay, I'm sorry. Please stop!" Avry cried out.

Within a blink of an eye, he sprung back up from the hole.

"That's better," Degg grunted. "You shouldn't be so ungrateful in a land so rich."

Charlie McFarley smirked as he watched Emelia struggling to pry her lips apart. "You'll have to see the rainbow to fix those lips," he said. "Now let's get ya to that grand prize that ye have been so fortunate to win. Just choose a path and stay positive, and the leprechauns will help you find yer way." Charlie clapped his hands three times, and the leprechauns disappeared.

Chapter 8
The Dancing Rainbow

Avry, Caitlyn, Trueman, and Emelia looked at each other strangely, while they stood in the middle of the two crossroads. Both pathways were identical, and there were no signs of the leprechauns from either direction. The Treelanders found themselves in a mystical green maze that dazzled and frightened them.

The tree vines on each side of the pathway appeared to dance to the rhythm of the lively Celtic music, consisting of bagpipes and flutes that still filled the air. Trueman began to smirk and giggled as he watched the tree vines hip-hop dance from side to side. Avry and Caitlyn began to laugh when Trueman's head began moving along with the rhythm of the vines.

"Do you like this song, Trueman?" Avry asked jokingly.

"Yeah, it's the answer," Trueman replied giddily. "The vines are dancing way over to the left."

Avry stared at the vines and then chuckled, "I see what you're talking about. Okay, let's go." Avry immediately started walking down the left path.

Everyone followed behind Avry with some hesitation. They walked for a while until they reached a three-way intersection. There was a low rumble overhead and a strange swishing sound like a ship crashing through waves. The Treelanders turned their attention to the sky and saw Slaughter's ship flying overhead. They could see Willow's face in the small hole on the ship's side and heard her scream when the ship passed by. Caitlyn immediately followed after the pirate ship and ran down the middle pathway.

"Caitlyn, wait!" Avry shouted, "It could just be a trick."

Caitlyn stopped and shrieked when clusters of trees fell to the ground blocking the path in front of her. She quickly ran back and joined the others.

"Caitlyn, I don't think that was the correct path," Avry said as he wiped sweat from his brow. There was a trace of sarcasm in his tone.

"Mmmmmm...mmmmm...," Emelia mumbled and pointed in every direction like she was playing a game of charades.

"Thanks for your help, Emelia," Caitlyn muttered, "but I think we can handle this without the extra drama."

Without warning, Degg, the leprechaun, fell from the sky into Emelia's arms. "Missy, Missy, you know the way, listen up everyone, Emelia has something to say," he sang with a childlike voice. "Oh, that's right; your lips are tied tight." He laughed so hard that he fell onto the ground. He rolled around and kicked his little feet in the air.

Avry crossed his arms, and said to Degg, "Did I tell you that I think you are a—"

"Uh, uh, ahhhh...Avry you need to stay positive, for I have a clue," Degg said as he danced around in a circle. "They are black-and- white, could be day or night, one is wrong and one is right, only one will win a fight."

The silly leprechaun pointed to the two remaining paths. The one on the left turned pitch black and the one on the right turned cloudy bright white.

"Remember, you have all you need to succeed. Oops, there's another clue," Degg said and then disappeared.

"Come on, Caitlyn, you're great at figuring out riddles," Trueman cheered.

"Mmmmmmmmm!" Emelia continued to mumble and pointed straight up in the air.

"Let's see," Caitlyn said, thinking out loud with her index finger tapping her bottom lip. "Black is at night. It's not really white during the day, hmm...and obviously one path is wrong and one is right...but what wins a fight?"

"That's simple, a Treelander!" cried Trueman.

"Well, yes, but we are not black or white," Avry argued.

"You're right," Caitlyn said. "But a knight wins a fight—the good one white, and the bad one black."

"But what about the reference he made to day or night?" Avry asked.

"Yeah, and what did he mean, we 'have all we need to succeed?'" Trueman asked.

"Okay, well, let's look what we have to succeed with," Caitlyn said in a shaky voice.

The Treelanders quickly dumped their belongings on the ground with a clang and a clatter.

"We've got swords, bows, and arrows to fight

with," said Caitlyn, "a bottle for giant swamp water…, Trueman's flute, in case we run into more slime, more green sand for Emelia to eat later, if she ever gets her mouth open again…, Avry's looking glass, and…Avry, where did you get this?" She held up Captain Slaughter's black metal glove.

"It kind of just slipped off Slaughter's hand, I guess." Avry said matter-of-fact-like, "I'm not really sure why I kept it though."

"All right, well, that only leaves one thing…the starlight map," Caitlyn concluded.

Emelia struggled to pry open her lips and mumbled loudly, "MMMMMMM!"

Caitlyn clapped her hands in triumph (so she thought). "That's it! We need the starlight map to see in the darkness. It's got to be the dark path."

Avry grabbed the starlight map and looked down the dark path. "*AAAAAAAAAAAAAAAAAAAHHH*!" he screamed.

"What is it?" Trueman asked and began to tremble.

"I don't think that's the right way!" Avry screeched. "There's a very large hairy leprechaun, with fangs and glowing red eyes, walking this way!"

"Well, look down the other path then!" Caitlyn begged.

Avry put the starlight map up to his eye and looked down the path to his left. A beam of light shot out of the map, down the white, glowing path, and then bounced back and drove Avry backward.

"What was that, Avry?" Trueman cried, his knees shaking and knocking like clapping hands.

"I couldn't see anything, just the same glowing white that you can see, except brighter, like the sun."

"Well, I say we go down the white path," Trueman said, biting his lip.

The Treelanders all agreed and began to jog down the glowing white path. The music suddenly stopped the minute they stepped on the path and the only thing they could hear was a soft humming sound.

"This is a strange place," Caitlyn whispered. "And just for the record, I don't like mazes."

"Yeah, but this has to be the right way," Trueman said, panting.

The Treelanders walked down the path for a long time—a very long time—and continued to listen to the humming sound that only grew louder.

"My feet are getting tired, and I'm getting dizzy from that sound," Trueman whined.

POP! A loud, squishing thud echoed around them.

Oscar, the leprechaun, appeared in front of the Treelanders. They stopped dead in their tracks, trying to avoid a freakish sight. Oscar's head, and only his head, levitated back and forth in front of them. His body was nowhere to be seen.

"Very simple, you see," Oscar's head said. "Hands and feet are all you need to succeed." His head spun around three hundred and sixty degrees and then he continued. "Oh, and if you see my body anywhere, please tell it to meet me at the gate."

Oscar's head vanished out of sight, the glowing path grew darker, and the tree vines began to form an arc over their heads. The sliver of blue sky disappeared. Avry, Trueman, Caitlyn, and Emelia jolted away from the flurry of loud footsteps that approached them. The pathway shook with each pounding pulse and continued to get louder as every second passed. Foul hot air, like stale morning breath, rushed down the dark pathway behind the Treelanders. Avry reached for the starlight map, and a beam of light shot down the trail in front of them, revealing Oscar's headless body that held a large, spiked club in its hand. The headless body smashed the pathway with the club, sending the pathway crumbling into the ground.

"This doesn't look good; we have to figure out the riddle," Avry said. He began to shake like Trueman.

Avry turned the beam of light toward the path behind them. The light landed on the large, hairy, wolf-like leprechaun, with red eyes bulging outward and gleaming from the ray of light. Drool dripped from its large slime-covered green teeth; snots oozed and bubbled from its crooked nose; and hot, steamy air blew toward the Treelanders with every grunt it made.

Caitlyn tried to stay calm while she worked out the riddle, "Hands...Feet...oh...!"

Avry took his bow and arrow out and fired an arrow straight into the evil leprechaun's chest. It growled louder and became enraged.

"Grrr!" The monstrous leprechaun roared. The arrow stuck into its chest, and it proceeded to approach them with no ill effect. Dark, crude blood gushed from the monster's chest like a small fountain. It pulled the arrow out effortlessly and turned the bloody weapon into tiny splinters of dust.

"Hands, feet are all we need...Quick, Avry, shine the light straight up!" Caitlyn shouted and tried to catch her breath. "That's it...all we have to do is climb out of here."

Both the headless and the wolf-like leprechauns approached the Treelanders, while they raced up the clover-covered tree vines.

"Quick, climb faster!" Avry shouted. His heart pounded in his chest, "They're getting closer!"

The wolf-like leprechaun jumped up and dug its sharp claws into Trueman's left leg.

"Somebody help me!" Trueman howled in agony. He tried to slash the mutant leprechaun with his sword, but it seemed to have no effect. The monster's nails had penetrated into Trueman's skin and clutched him even tighter.

Trueman screeched and kicked the monster. Tears streamed down the boy's face and his lips quivered. It felt to Trueman like the wolf-like leprechaun was about to grind his leg bone into powder if it didn't stop squeezing.

Avry shot arrows down at the monster from above and stuck the wolf-like creature in one of its eyes. Blood gurgled out from its eye socket, and the monster squealed in pain. The evil leprechaun slashed at Trueman's pants and tore them to shreds.

"Avry, Help me! This thing is going to kill me!" Trueman hollered. His heart was now in his throat.

Then seemingly without any reason at all, the

wolf-like leprechaun released its grip. The Treelanders just stared in awe for a moment and then quickly continued to hike higher and higher until they could almost see the bright blue sky through the vines. Avry took the starlight map and looked down at the two mutant leprechauns.

Avry took a deep breath, "Look, Trueman, it was Oscar's body that saved you."

The headless leprechaun was beating the wolf-like leprechaun into the ground. It screamed, snorted, and flailed about on the ground like a dying pig.

"Wow, talk about having a bad day," Trueman snickered with some relief.

The Treelanders continued to climb to the top of the extremely high trees. When they reached the top, Caitlyn slashed a hole through the tangled, knotted vines with her sword to expose the open blue sky.

The sun was shining brightly, the birds were singing, and the Treelanders could finally see the pot of gold. Over in a large field surrounded by a white picket fence stood an oversize golden pot with gold coins that flowed out and spread into the long green grass. Diamonds, pearls, rubies, and silver coins hung from trees that surrounded the golden pot. A colorful rainbow shook and danced in the center of the pot and arced upward and outward to another land.

The Treelanders floated down to the field where Charlie McFarley, Degg, and Oscar's head stood next to a gate, waiting for the Treelanders' arrival.

"You're here! You're here! You're here and finally done! Take anything here you want, but you may only take just one," Charlie sang with glee.

Caitlyn smiled and put her hand on the leprechaun's shoulder, saying, "Thank you very much Charlie, but all we want is to find Raider and get back the dragon egg."

"Well then, it's not every day that you find the pot of gold at the end of a rainbow." Charlie's smile was almost electric, his teeth stretched from ear to ear. "However, it's not every day that you get to talk to a rainbow and get your wish."

Charlie opened the gate to the field and pointed at the rainbow, "Right this way, the rainbow will be happy to help you with your request."

The Treelanders walked over to the rainbow that was singing and dancing in the pot of gold. "You've made it to the end of the rainbow, to find your pot of gold. Gold is rich and happy, for the poor, young and old," it sang.

"Uh...excuse me, Mister Rainbow," Caitlyn cleared her throat. "We are looking for a sea monkey carrying a beautiful dragon egg. Have you seen him?"

The rainbow continued to dance and sing. "La, la, la. Sea monkey, oh yes, to get across my rainbow bridge, the question you must guess. Oh, and please call me Ray!"

"I am so sick and tired of riddles and songs," Avry groaned.

"But young man, it's a very simple riddle, and one of you will surely answer correctly," Ray said.

"Go ahead, we will listen to your riddle," Caitlyn

muttered. She crossed her arms, and rolled her eyes.

"Very well, here goes," Ray began. "What's sweet to eat and flies through the air? They are light on their feet and have glowing white hair."

"MMMMMMMMMMMMMMMMMMMM!" Emelia moaned loudly.

Emelia began to run around in circles and stomp her feet; she grabbed sand from the ground and threw it in the air, flapping her arms and wings like a giant bird.

"It figures she's the one who knows the answer," Trueman mumbled.

"Great. Can someone here please fix her lips?" Avry cried impatiently. There was no question in his statement.

"Avry, she is giving us clues," Caitlyn snapped.

"Oh, I thought she was just a crazy loony bird," Avry grumbled.

"You're a bird?" Trueman guessed. He flapped his arms and wings.

Emelia shook her head left and right three times and threw more green sand in the air.

Trueman jumped up and down, "Oh, I've got it. You're a sand bird with blonde hair."

Emelia stomped her feet out of frustration.

"Well, this is going well," Avry said sarcastically. "It looks like we are going to be here for a while—" A soft hiss made him pause. He listened to it grow louder. "Hey, what's that noise?"

They were all startled by the loud whistling that bellowed from Avry's backpack. Avry swung his backpack to the ground as if it was a wild animal attacking him. He carefully pulled back and opened the flap on the pack to locate the whistling predator. "It's the map," he said, surprised. Avry put the end of the starlight map up to his eye. He felt like he was flying through space while he looked into the tube until he saw Zia standing next to Jewlz at the lake under the great falls. It gave him the illusion that he was standing there with them.

"Avry, you must hurry, Jewlz is very sick and dying," Zia's tired and raspy voice reverberated from the map. The others listened. "King Oliver is also missing; he was abducted by something last night," the witch's voice quivered. "Oh, and one more thing…the fire and ice curse is changing; the flames are dying out."

"Great," Avry exclaimed, "we keep running into problems, Zia, and right now we need a little help."

"I can see you need help," Zia retorted. "Well, I can help you with Emelia's lip problem, but she will have to answer the riddle. You all must eat the first thing that Emelia ate this morning. Now hurry please!"

The map went black, and Zia was gone.

"Well, that's great; we didn't eat anything this morning," Trueman fussed.

"Oh yes, we did," Caitlyn said with a scowl. "Emelia ate the green sand on the beach, remember?"

"We have plenty of green sand right here in the field," Ray said happily. The rainbow danced and shook and then a small hand stretched from the tall, colorful arc. A small, multicolored finger pointed to the field.

Avry walked over to the green sand and picked up a large handful, he handed some to Trueman and Caitlyn and said, "Start eating. I want to get out of here," he tossed back a handful of the sandy grit into his gullet.

"Hey, this is not too bad," Trueman said, licking his sprinkled green lips.

Emelia started to mumble, "mmmmMMMM!"

"How much sand do we have to eat for this to work?" Avry asked. "Wait a minute, Caitlyn, you need to eat that!" he shouted.

Caitlyn put the sand up to her lips and pretended to eat it. Her jaw bounced up and down and chomped at the air. "But I don't like—"

"EAT IT!" Avry shouted.

"Alright, you don't have to get so upset."

Caitlyn made a sour-looking face and ate the sand. She crossed her eyes when she swallowed it and stuck out her green-coated tongue at Avry.

"Well, it's about time," Emelia growled through gritted teeth. "I thought I was going to have to draw out the answer in the sand with your face, Caitlyn."

"Not all of us like lime-flavored sand," Caitlyn whined.

"Do you have the answer to my riddle, young Emelia?" Ray asked.

"Yeah, it's simple—sugarplumb fairies," Emelia said with a smile.

The colors on the rainbow shined brighter and Ray jumped and danced in the golden pot. "You've answered correctly, so waste no time, step right up, and step inside," he sang.

A large rainbow-colored ladder extended down from the top of the golden pot, and a small door opened at the end of the rainbow.

The Treelanders quickly climbed the ladder to the top of the golden pot. They waved to Charlie McFarley, Degg, and Oscar's head, then stepped inside the door while Ray continued to sing, "Sit right back and enjoy the ride of surprises and colors to the other side."

The door whooshed shut, and they were on their way, perhaps moving closer to the land of the giants. It didn't seem to matter too much, they were moving, and that was better than being stuck in a crazy maze.

Inside the rainbow, the walls were colorful and transparent. The Treelanders could see clearly outside as the floor began to elevate upward through the rainbow center. Their voices bounced off the glasslike walls and echoed through the rainbow tube when they shouted in amazement.

"Hey, look, there's Charlie!" Trueman yelled, "Oh, and Oscar got his body back."

"Wait! Who's that?!" Emelia pointed in the distance.

"Go back!" Caitlyn commanded to the rainbow. "It's that person who's been following us in the black-hooded cloak. He's talking to Charlie. Willow was right! I feel so bad that I didn't listen to her in the first place."

"I'm sorry," Ray said deeply, "but some people don't even get one trip to the pot of gold. Consider yourselves lucky that you made it there. We will be at the top of the rainbow in just a few minutes; please hold on tightly."

Avry scratched his forehead with his index finger and asked, "I wonder why that person was talking to Charlie, and why would he be following us?"

"Maybe he works for the giants and keeps making all this bad stuff happen to us," Emelia replied.

While the Treelanders continued to discuss the mysterious figure, the floor raised them higher toward the top of the rainbow. Beneath the rainbow, a large lake stretched to a forbidden land they had yet to explore.

"How long before we get to the other side?" Emelia asked.

Ray cleared his throat, which echoed loudly in the rainbow tube. "I'm afraid we need to slow down; there is trouble below." The Treelanders covered their ears as his hollow voice lingered in the air.

Loud explosions from cannon fire blasted under the rainbow. The rainbow tube vibrated with each blast and the rising elevator continued to slow down as they neared the top. The Treelanders quickly looked underneath themselves to watch the chaos.

Avry looked through the starlight map to get a better look. "It's Raider! Captain Slaughter and his men are chasing Raider. Wait, look. There's Willow. She's yelling at one of the pirates...ouch!"

Emelia tugged on Avry's shoulder and asked, "What is it, Avry?"

"Well," he paused to snort, "I guess you could say the pirates can't be too happy to have Willow on board. She just bit one of them on the arm."

"Serves them right," Caitlyn cheered. "She's a feisty one, and they are in for a big surprise."

"Excuse me, Mister Rainbow, but can you take us down there?" Trueman asked.

"No, I'm sorry, but you will like the beautiful land that we are traveling to," Ray's voice echoed.

Captain Slaughter's ship had disappeared beneath the water once again in search of Raider. The Treelanders continued to move slowly upward until they reached the highest part of the rainbow. A small rainbow-striped boat waited at the top for the Treelanders to board.

"Climb in, kids, and hold on," Ray called out.

Water flowed down the other side of the rainbow center. The Treelanders wasted no time jumping into the boat. The candy- striped float carried them down the rainbow tube at a chilling speed. Beams of colored lights passed their eyes as they bolted down the tube.

"Wow! This is amazing!" Caitlyn screamed.

"Yeah, we've got to build one of these back home," Trueman added.

"Did I mention I'm hungry?" Emelia groaned.

Avry shook his head, pointing forward, and said, "Try to have a little fun without eating for a change, Emelia."

The Treelanders soared faster and faster down through the red, blue, green, yellow, orange, and pink tube. The colors swirled and turned into other amazing shades of color.

"I think I'm going to be sick," Emelia wailed.

"Yeah, this is awesome!" Avry shouted. "Just don't get sick on me." His face went sour.

"These colors are amazing!" Caitlyn yelled.

A blinding neon light flashed before their eyes, and the sound of rushing water grew increasingly loud as they reached the bottom of the rainbow.

Splash! Water and mud exploded into the air and crashed down on the Treelanders. The boat flooded as the front nose-dived, and the boat screeched to a halt. The kids were tossed through the air and landed in a large, soupy green pond.

Chapter 9
The Mushroom Harp

The Treelanders stood drenched up to their waists in a small pond that was mostly covered with large green lily pads. Mud had speckled their faces like a wild outbreak of brown measles. Red and yellow flowers surrounded the water's edge, and a large weeping willow tree hung over a small sparkling stream that trickled into the pond. Large blue geese grazed through the pondweed and stared at the Treelanders, while they climbed out of the soupy green water. A large goose honked and charged at Emelia who was eating some pondweed. The goose pecked on her head, grabbed the pondweed, and flew back to join the other geese.

"Ouch! Can't anyone get something to eat around here? I'm hungry!" Emelia rubbed the back of her head.

Caitlyn gave Emelia a shove, "You deserved that, Emelia. Be patient, we'll eat soon."

Plush green grass covered the ground surrounded by an enormous bountiful garden of beautiful flowers and fruit plants. In the middle of the garden, on top of a small grass-covered hill, stood an oversized red mushroom covered with white spots. Silver strings stretched to the ground from beneath the head of the polka-dotted mushroom, and soft tender music played from the harp.

Trueman began to dance and pulled out his

flute, “Wow! I hear the music, but no one is playing the harp.”

“Probably just another trick by the leprechauns,” Emelia said grumpily. “Now put that stupid thing away.”

Soft giggles came from behind the fruit plants, and a small faerie with blonde hair slowly raised her head from behind the mushroom harp. Her soft, tender wings fluttered, while she hovered above the mushroom. Her face was pretty and sparkled silver. She laughed at Avry when he fell backward at the sight of her.

“H-h-he-hello,” Avry stuttered, as he brushed himself off.

“Welcome to the faerie garden. My name is Nire, and these are my friends,” she said, pointing to the plants.

More giggles continued from behind the plants, which shook with excitement.

“Don’t worry, we won’t hurt you,” Emelia said sweetly, peeking at a faerie that was hidden behind a batch of yellow tulips.

Dozens of elegant faeries began to rise up from behind the flowers and wafted into the air. The mushroom harp played louder and filled the air with a warm melody.

“Is this fruit okay to eat?” Emelia asked excitedly.

“Please, everyone, help yourselves to our garden,” Nire invited.

Emelia and the others immediately grabbed whatever fruit was in front of them and began to feast.

"I've never tasted anything so good!" Emelia exclaimed, as she bit into a juicy peach.

"It's because your last meal was sand," Caitlyn said with a snarl.

Nire glided over toward Avry and sat down next to him. "Have you traveled long?"

Avry just stared at Nire with his mouth wide open and speechless.

"You could say it's been too long," Trueman said and then bit into two oversized apples at once.

Avry's starry eyes glistened, and he answered, "Yeah—um—well, we are looking for something. That's why we ended up here." He continued to stare at Nire with a goofy smile.

A faerie with red hair and a lavender dress flew down next to Avry.

"I bet I know what you're looking for," the faerie taunted.

"Quiet down, Ali. These people don't want to be bothered by your games," Nire said harshly.

Trueman walked around the mushroom and squinted curiously, "Hey...how does this harp play by itself?"

"This is the magical mushroom harp of harmony," Nire replied proudly. "It provides us faeries with magic and protection."

"Ali, you started to mention that you knew what we are looking for," Caitlyn interrupted.

Nire held up her dainty hand, saying, "People come through here all the time looking for things that the rainbow throws back, and then Ali makes them try to find it in the pond. Sometimes it is pretty *funny to watch people look for hours in the place* that it is not."

Avry brushed back his disheveled hair and wiped his mouth clean. "Well, we've been chasing after a dragon egg that belongs to us, and this sea monkey named Raider has stolen it for the giants."

The faeries all began to laugh hard at Avry's story.

"Why are you laughing?" Caitlyn asked. Her eyebrows frowned and her cheeks grew puffy. "Our people could die if we don't get that egg back."

An older-looking faerie with white hair flew over to Emelia and pulled the fruit out of her hands. Emelia stood with her mouth wide open while she looked at her empty palms. The faerie tossed the fruit into a large patch of sunflowers where butterflies and bees rested. The disturbed insects swarmed around in a circle above their heads.

"Good throw, Krista!" Ali shouted with a giggle.

The faeries spun through the air and laughed while Emelia went chasing after the fruit.

"Hey! Why did you do that?" Emelia yelled, as she swatted bees away from her face.

"Maybe because you've had about twenty pieces of fruit already," Caitlyn muttered.

"Well, I haven't tried that one yet," Emelia grunted whiled she crawled into the sunflower patch to get the fruit. She began to mumble to herself while she crawled on her hands and knees further into the sunflower patch, "They think it's funny, ha ha. Maybe if they were hungry and I took their food, and I...OUCH!" She bumped her head on a large object and couldn't believe her eyes when she looked at what stood in her path.

"Avry, Caitlyn, Trueman! Come quick!" she cried.

"Now what?" Avry spat, as he rolled his eyes.

Everyone ran toward Emelia's wincing voice. Avry, Caitlyn, and Trueman pushed their way through the tall sunflower plants to find their sister. When they got to the center of the sunflower patch, they stood in amazement. Emelia was sitting on the ground eating a piece of fruit and gazing up at the dragon egg that was perched in a small nest. Rings of water spun around the egg as it shined and shimmered from the setting sun.

"Is this an illusion or is this our dragon egg?" Avry asked.

Juice ran down Emelia's chin as she chomped away on the fruit saying, "I don't know...but whatever this fruit is, it is amazing."

"Yes, Avry," Krista answered. "This is the egg that you have been looking for and this is no illusion."

Trueman mouthed a word several times until he asked, "How did it get here, and what happened to Raider?"

"Ray always throws things back from the pot of gold, and we make sure that they go to their rightful owners," Nire said. "When we saw Raider looking for the egg, we knew right away that it wasn't his. So we hid it here and protected it with the aquaflect rings. Even if Raider did find it, he couldn't take it."

"But what happened to Raider?" Emelia asked

the unanswered question again. "He doesn't give up that easily, ya know."

"Our magic is no match for that silly sea monkey," Krista replied.

Ali flew about and giggled, leaving a trail of silver dust around Emelia's head, and said, "You could say we sent him on a wild goose chase."

Nire flew over and sat on Emelia's shoulder, adding, "Ali painted a ball to look like the egg and then she made it roll away. Raider ran after it, and we haven't seen him since." The faerie flew into the air and burst into laughter.

Trueman's eyes had never been so big when he said, "Do you know what this means, guys? All we need now is Willow...the giant swamp water, and then we can go home!"

"Yeah, I wish there was some way to tell Zita and Zia," Avry mumbled.

Emelia stood up, reached in Avry's backpack, and handed him the starlight map, saying, "Avry, why don't you try using this."

Avry nodded, took the map, and looked up to the sky. A detailed map of where they had traveled appeared before his eyes, but there was no sign of Zia or Zita. Avry put one end of the rolled-up map to his mouth and began yelling into the tube, "Zia! Zita! Are you there? Hello! We found the egg! Can you hear me?"

"You do know how ridiculous you look, don't you?" Caitlyn said with a chuckle.

"Well, we've got to let them know somehow," Avry said.

"Zia and Zita used to live over there in the auburn hills," Ali said matter-of-factly.

"That was a long time ago, Ali, even before Kildane was around," Krista corrected her.

"What's a Kildane?" Trueman asked curiously. "Is that like a burlybeast or something?"

Krista flew over to Trueman and poked him in the nose, saying, "Not what, but who. Kildane is a powerful warlock who lives in a cave up in the auburn hills. He has used his evil magic to wreak havoc all over the forbidden land, and some say he even controls the giants."

"What made Zia and Zita leave there?" Avry asked.

"The giants and Kildane tormented the people in the forbidden land," Nire replied. "Kildane brought the leprechauns, the pirates, and us here from another world. Kildane had cast evil spells on the people of New Gander. Zia and Zita went to New Gander to help save some of the villagers and brought them to the kingdom of Epalushia."

"I r-r-really don't want to meet that guy," Trueman trembled.

"You don't have to worry about him. You'll be safe here," Ali said reassuringly.

"Well, we need to get to the giants' swamp and get some water to help cure our people," Avry said, putting the map in his backpack.

"Yeah, and don't forget Willow," said Caitlyn.

"Don't worry. I haven't forgotten. We'll get her back too," Avry chuckled.

"It will take almost a full day to get to the giants'

swamp," Krista said. "You may stay here tonight and rest if you wish."

Avry looked up to the night sky as the thirteen moons shone brightly upon him, casting a blue glow on his olive skin. "Well, it has been a long day...We'll stay the night and then leave first thing in the morning."

"Very good. You can sleep in the hollow room inside the weeping willow tree," Nire said, pointing to her right.

"No, thanks. I'd be more comfortable sleeping on the ground right next to the dragon egg," Avry smirked.

Krista shook her head, her hair floating softly in the breeze, and said, "You have nothing to worry about...I can assure you the egg will be safe here with the aquaflect."

"I don't know," Avry thought. "We've come a long way...to leave it here while we sleep somewhere else..."

"If you don't believe me, then try to take the egg," Krista said boldly.

Avry walked up to the egg and watched as the rings of water spun around the egg. He slowly reached his hands in between two spinning rings of electric liquid. His hands began to vibrate as they approached the egg's shell. Suddenly an arc of electricity came out of the rings of water and shocked Avry's hands. The shock catapulted Avry backward through the air and into the pond behind him.

Everyone laughed at Avry, as he shook his long wet hair and pulled himself out of the water. He rolled his eyes and then smirked, "Okay, I get the point. We will sleep in the willow tree." He laughed in spite of himself.

"Very well, then. Right this way," Nire said, as she continued to bellow with laughter.

The Treelanders followed Nire to the large weeping willow and entered through a small hole on the side of the timber. Nire and the group of the faeries flew up onto the willow braches and rested for the night.

The mushroom harp continued to play softly into the hours of darkness, while the Treelanders settled into their room—a room with beds made of hay buried deep inside the splendid hollow. They put their minds to ease for the moment and fell fast asleep—well, almost everyone.

Chapter 10
Kildane's Ghosts

It was just after midnight, and everybody inside the willow tree was asleep except for Trueman, who lay awake, troubled, and restless. He couldn't stop worrying about Willow (his sister, not the tree), he missed his parents, and more importantly at that moment, he was frightened of the dark. There were no jars of fireflies or campfires like he had back home to brighten the dark room. He was terrified of the pitch black, and no one would wake up to talk to him.

Outside, the mushroom harp played a gentle lullaby melody into the still night air. But even the music didn't help Trueman fall asleep. He nudged Avry on the shoulder to wake him up, but Avry just growled and rolled over. Caitlyn and Emelia talked in their sleep, and it frightened Trueman even more when they mumbled a lot of loud nonsense words like "Beware...co...wiz...ard."

Trueman rolled over and began to fumble his hand around on the floor. His fingernails scratched at the wooden floor while he wrestled and reached for Avry's bag. "Now, where is that starlight map?" he whispered to himself.

Trueman rummaged through the backpack and talked to himself out loud. "Ouch! That's not it...arrow...what's this? Nope, that's Avry's looking glass. Aha!"

A beam of light filled the room as soon as Trueman put the starlight map up to his eye. "That's better. Now I can sleep," he thought to himself.

"What are you doing, Trueman," Avry mumbled groggily.

"I can't sleep. It's too dark in here."

"Put that light out and go to sleep. We have a big day tomorrow."

Avry rolled over and went back to sleep. Trueman continued to play with the starlight map. He shined it on the walls and saw beautiful carved pictures of the faeries and their garden. He looked inside the rolled-up map and saw a small hole at the top of the tree. The beam of light shot out into the starry night. Stars twisted and swirled into a detailed map of where the Treelanders had once traveled. The stars formed into pictures of Treeland, Sky Lake, Coral Mountain, the land of the leprechauns, and the faerie garden.

Trueman looked even closer at the map of stars; he studied the land of the faeries and even more details formed before his eyes. Clusters of stars blossomed into the large weeping willow tree that hung over a small brook, as well as the red and white polka-dotted mushroom harp.

Trueman continued to talk to himself, "This thing is so cool! Hey, I wonder if I can see the egg? WOW...There it is. Hey, who are they?"

Two strange figures appeared on the map, and then the vision went black. "What's wrong with this thing?" Trueman yelled and shook the map up and down.

Outside, dark clouds covered the stars and the mushroom harp played a loud and piercing song. Heavy rain started to pour down on the faerie garden. A strong gust of wind blew inside the willow tree and almost knocked Trueman over; he poked his head outside and gulped, "Avry, come quick!" His heart pounded hard in chest, and his insides turned cold.

Avry poked one eye open and said in a scratchy voice, "Trueman, come back to bed. It's just a rain storm."

Trueman couldn't speak; he barely managed to get out a word, saying, "N-n-no, it's NOT!"

Trueman ducked out of the way from a white owl that flew straight through him. "Th-th-they're not real!" Trueman shrilled. "G-g- ghosts!"

Four more ghost-like owls flew through the walls of the tree and startled Avry, Caitlyn, and Emelia. Everyone rushed outside into the pouring rain, screaming from the attack of ghost owls.

"Trueman, what's going on out here!?" Caitlyn screamed.

"There's somebody over by the egg," Trueman replied.

All the faeries flew down from the willow tree to the fruit garden. A few of them chased after the ghost owls, and Nire, Ali, and Krista flew over to the sunflower patch.

"Somebody's trying to steal the egg!" Avry shouted as he ran toward the sunflower patch.

The rain and wind grew stronger and was blinding. A sudden bolt of lighting shot out from the sunflower patch, and Raider went flying backward into Avry, sending them both crashing to the ground.

Avry quickly jumped to his feet and wiped blood from his lip. His wild hair tossed around in the breeze like serpents. He sneered and clenched his fists. "You're not getting that egg back this time, Raider!" he said with a growl. Avry couldn't resist the urge and jumped onto Raider, punching him—over and over, yelling with every hit. Raider kicked Avry in the stomach and Avry rolled over, wincing and wheezing.

"Out of my way, tree bird," Raider grumbled. "You are no match for Raider and Kildane."

Raider turned and ran immediately back toward the sunflower patch. Trueman, Caitlyn, and Emelia ran over to Avry, who was still rolled up in a ball on the ground.

Avry held his stomach and panted, "Kildane...is...here, and he's without a doubt helping Raider steal the...egg."

"Oh boy, I really did not want to meet this guy," Trueman shuddered.

Avry forced himself up, saying, "We have to help the faeries stop them from taking our egg. Let's go."

The Treelanders ran into the patch of sunflowers, and more sparks of lightning shot up into the air. When the Treelanders got closer to the middle of the flower patch, they saw Raider attempting to steal the egg. The aquaflect electric barrier stood strong and faithful to its well-kept dragon egg. Raider proceeded cautiously but was unsuccessful, as he reached several times for the precious egg. The results were always the same—shock, zap, and blisters.

Standing next to Raider was a very tall figure in a brown hooded robe. The robe had gold trim that glittered, and the figure wore a black glossy mask that covered his face. It was Kildane, the warlock. The evil magician had already cast a spell on the faeries to keep them away from the egg. He held his hand up toward the helpless faeries, and a pulse of blue light kept pushing Nire, Ali, and Krista backward.

Kildane's frustration escalated, and he began to fume at his puppet, the week pathetic sea monkey. He said, "Just take the egg! Get it NOW!"

"But, Master Kildane, the faerie spell is too strong. Look at my burning hands," Raider whined. His hands had become black and charred from the hot electric shock of the aquaflect.

"Krista, I order you to remove the aquaflect spell at once!" Kildane commanded.

"You will not get me or any of the faerie folk to help you with your greed for gold," Krista shouted. "The egg does not belong to you. It belongs to the Treelanders!"

"That's right, Kildane, it belongs to us!" Avry shouted with pride.

"Yeah, and there's four of us and only two of you," Caitlyn growled. "So why don't you leave now, if you know what's good for you?"

"You Treelanders should go home before I teach you a lesson," Kildane said, as he snapped his head back and laughed hysterically.

Raider also began to laugh, showing off his sharp green teeth that dripped with slime.

"We're not going anywhere!" Emelia said, and she charged at Kildane.

Avry and Caitlyn rushed behind Emelia toward the warlock, while Trueman crouched behind a bush. Kildane held his golden cane up into the air. A flock of ghost owls spun down from the sky like a tornado and pulled the Treelanders into the air. The other faeries flew over to help the kids while they spun in the funnel of ghost owls.

Kildane held up a devilish fist to the faeries, saying, "Krista, I am warning you for the last time—remove the spell."

Krista pulled out her wand and aimed it at the egg. She began to mumble a curse as she waved the wand through the air. A stream of fire exploded out of her wand and traveled toward the egg. Just before the fire hit the egg it turned and struck Raider's spiked orange hair. Trueman began to laugh, as Raider rolled around on the ground and tried to douse the fire.

"Trueman, help us!" Caitlyn cried.

"Kildane—put us down!" Avry shouted. He had become nauseated from the spinning and wasn't sure how much more he could take.

The warlock spun his gold cane around in circles and the Treelanders began to spin higher into the air.

Trueman peered out of the bushes; his hands shook as he grabbed his bow and arrow. He cocked the long wooden arrow way back on his bow, aimed straight at Kildane, and fired the feathered spear into Kildane's back.

The ghost owls disappeared the minute the arrow stuck into Kildane. Weightless for just a second, the Treelanders spun downward through the air toward the chaos on the ground. The faeries had also been released of their spell, as Kildane struggled to pull the bloody arrow out of his back.

"Ahhh...you pesky little twerp, you will pay for this!" Kildane winced. His voice gave a faint hint of the pain he was in.

Kildane grabbed his gold cane and spiked it into the muddy ground. It sank deep into the mud and gleamed into a fiery orange staff. An enormous bolt of blue lightning shot down from the sky and sent sparks out the end of the newly created fire staff. Hundreds, maybe even thousands, of ghost owls spewed out the end of the cane and pulled the faeries and the Treelanders—including Trueman—back into the air.

"Now you faeries will pay for not helping me!" Kildane groaned. Then he quickly grabbed his cane, ran over to the mushroom harp, pulled the strings off the harp, and wrapped them around his golden cane.

The rings of water for the Aquaflect vanished; Raider immediately grabbed the dragon egg and fled once again; the ghost owls dropped the faeries and Treelanders onto the muddy ground below; and finally, the swarm of eerie creatures picked up their master and disappeared out of sight.

The rain stopped abruptly and everything became very silent. The Treelanders and the faeries—covered in mud—pulled themselves up off the ground and stood baffled.

Caitlyn wiped mud from her eyes and said, "Why was Kildane helping Raider and what did he want with the egg?"

"Kildane must be helping the giants," Ali replied in tears. "This can't be good..." She broke off into sobs.

"I couldn't see a thing," Emelia said, as she licked the mud off her lips. "Mmm—why did Kildane take off in such a hurry?"

"Trueman shot him with an arrow," Nire replied, tears streaming down her dull cheeks.

"I knew you had it in you, little brother," Avry said. He hugged Trueman and smiled.

"Hey, listen...the music stopped," Trueman said with a frown.

"Yes, I'm afraid Kildane has taken the magical strings to our mushroom harp," Krista said, swallowing back her sorrow. "Without the magic strings...there is no music. And with no music...there is no magic for us faeries."

"What do you mean?" Avry cocked his head. "I'm confused," he said, as he shrugged his shoulders.

"We can't fly or perform any magic unless we get those strings back," Krista said grimly.

"But Kildane is too powerful, Krista. How can we get the strings back?" Trueman asked.

"Are you saying you will help us get the strings

back before you go after the egg?" Nire asked.

Avry nodded, "We are responsible for this mess; if the egg wasn't here, Kildane would never have come to this peaceful garden. So, yes, we would be happy to help you get the magic strings back."

"But, Avry, we don't know magic, and our weapons are no match for Kildane," Emelia said. "Besides, we don't even know how to find him."

Krista motioned to fly and then stumbled forward. Her sad and dull face looked toward the hills. She said, "My guess is that Kildane has vanished back to his cave on top of the auburn hills. Raider has the egg, so he's probably on his way to the giants. If you help us get our magic back we can help you reach the giants' swamp, as quick as you want."

"But, Krista, how are we going to defeat Kildane once we find him?" Caitlyn cried. "And why didn't you just send us to the swamp last night?"

"Well, it's not that easy, but..." Krista said, as she scratched her head and thought for a moment. She quickly ran over to the mushroom harp and pulled off the head of the mushroom. Inside the mushroom stem was a small, gray book. She picked it up and froze at the sight of the cover. The book that once sparkled with glitter had become dull and lifeless. She said, "Please excuse me, for my mind is getting old, and I have to refer to the faerie book of legends." She quickly turned the pages in the book. "I know there is a legend here that could help you..." The pages continued to turn and fan through her fingers, while everyone gathered around.

Chapter 11
The Ugly Stick

Krista's blue eyes widened as she said, "Let me see...Ah yes, here it is...*The Sword of the Knight.* Legend has it that Sir Taylor, the first knight to King Oliver, was sent to New Gander to protect the villagers from the giants. Taylor fought alongside his trusty dragon, named Sapphire, the second to the last living dragon in Epalushia. Together they defeated hundred of giants until one day, Kildane the warlock appeared and helped the giants with their battle. Taylor and Kildane fought a vicious war of magic against strength. Then it happened—Taylor struck Kildane with his sword and wounded the evil warlock. Kildane was furious because he knew that sword would kill him if it struck his heart. So in return, Kildane killed the dragon, cast a spell on the villagers of New Gander, and imprisoned Sir Taylor in his own sword."

"Wait a minute," Avry interrupted, "you said that Zia and Zita saved the people of New Gander."

"They came along shortly after Kildane had cast his spell on the villagers and had turned them into ugly sticks," Krista replied. "Zia and Zita were able to save some of the villagers that were hiding beneath the village and were not affected by the curse."

"Why did the knight's sword hurt Kildane?" Trueman asked.

"I'm not really sure," Krista shook her head. "You'll have to ask Zita. He gave the sword to Taylor."

"That's it!" Trueman cheered. "All we need is the sword and we can defeat Kildane!"

Krista smirked, "Yes, but to do so, you must go to New Gander and find the sword of the knight. It is hidden in the field of ugly sticks, and more importantly, you must choose correctly or you could also be turned into an ugly stick."

Ali nodded, "Yes, and as soon as you find the sword, you must go directly to the auburn hills to find and destroy Kildane."

"Krista, why were the giants and Kildane so persistent about tormenting the villagers in New Gander?" Avry asked curiously.

"Good question, Avry. Some say that they were after the burlybeasts, some say it was the gold, but I think they were after something King Oliver's brother, Arthur, had in his possession."

"But...why—what—who?" Trueman said, puzzled.

"Arthur and Oliver had a huge fight, so Arthur and some people from the kingdom of Epalushia came to this land and formed a village for people who didn't want to be dictated to by King Oliver any longer. It was a very peaceful and happy village like Treeland, I suppose. The people lived a charming and fruitful life."

"What was the brothers' fight about?" Caitlyn asked.

"The fight was over dictatorship and a woman, of course. Arthur fell in love with Queen Sheena and King Oliver became extremely jealous," Krista said, as she bit her bottom lip.

"Okay, but what does that have to do with the giants and Kildane?" Avry said, bothered.

"I'm getting to that," Krista continued. "Now let me finish. Kildane doesn't like anyone to be happy and he enjoys wreaking havoc on any peaceful land. So I suppose in the end, he decided that New Gander was a place to destroy. I don't think he ever found what Arthur had in his possession, either, because he continues to steal gold from all over Epalushia."

Trueman's head was bobbing left to right in a troubled manner. "Hey, where's Emelia?" he interrupted.

"Here I am!" Emelia exclaimed from behind a fruit plant.

Emelia continued to stuff her mouth with fruit as she poked her head out from the juicy red plants, "This story is boring me; you know, blah, blah, blah. Can't we just go now?"

Avry grinned sheepishly and said, "Rude but right, Emelia, we have a lot to do. I think we can hear more of this war and romance another time."

"One more thing," Nire said, pulling something from under the sash on her waist. "Take this bag of faerie dust and sprinkle it on the magic strings...once you get them back from Kildane, of course. The magic strings will transport you back here immediately."

Caitlyn looked puzzled and asked, "So, how do we get to New Gander?"

Nire pointed to a small dirt path, "Just take

this north path to the desert and you will find New Gander."

The Treelanders filled their bags with fruit, said good-bye to the faeries, and headed down the narrow dirt path. Violet flowers filled the fields on each side of the path. The smooth sweet flowery smell was inviting yet overwhelming. They traveled for hours until the morning sun had come up in the distance, revealing the auburn hills. Strange white birds with long wings and thin, pointed beaks flew over their heads.

"Those guys have the right idea; I'd rather be flying than walking," Emelia complained.

"I would rather be flying too, Emelia, but there are no large trees to climb and jump from. I'm sure it won't be long before we get to New Gander," Avry said as he began to pick up the pace.

A rush of sand flew into the air from the path in front of them. The Treelanders heard the familiar sound of burlybeasts.

"Wow, Avry, it almost sounds like back home," Trueman said in almost a whisper.

"Yeah, let's go!" Avry replied and ran quickly down the path and out of sight from the others.

Caitlyn, Emelia, and Trueman chased after Avry through the yellow cloud of dust that he stirred from the ground. When they caught up to him, they found him standing and staring with his mouth wide open. He gazed out upon a large field of sticks that stood straight up out of the sandy ground. The twisted and knotted sticks were thin on the bottom and grew thicker toward the top. The brown, wooden, bent rods looked like an army—a dead army—dressed to kill. The bark covering on the wooden sticks was wrinkled, bubbled, and covered with fury moss. They seemed to look at the kids in a way that made them feel like the sticks were going to attack them at any second. Avry felt his stomach roll over and twist in knots.

The deserted village of New Gander stood behind the barren sea of ugly sticks. The wind howled—eerie ghostly whines. The village that some called paradise was now a ghost town that lay in ruin. Two large burlybeasts wandered through the ghost town and fled immediately when they heard Caitlyn's voice saying, "How are we suppose to choose the right stick? There are too many ugly sticks to choose from." Her voice trailed off into a whining sigh.

Erie hollow voices emerged from the field of sticks. The voices started off soft and then grew very loud, "Pick me! No, PICK ME! I REALLY INSIST YOU PICK ME! Don't listen to her PICK ME!"

Avry rubbed his eyes; he stood dumbfounded, as small wooden mouths moved up and down at the top of the ugly sticks.

"H-H-Hello," Trueman called hesitantly.

One of the sticks closest to Trueman shouted, "I am the knight that you seek!"

"Trueman, no...!" Avry hollered. He reached out to stop Trueman from touching the stick but he was too late. Trueman's backpack fell to the ground around an ugly stick that replaced Trueman's body. Avry watched in disbelief, as a tiny wooden knotted mouth began to move. "Avry—help me! I don't want to be a stick!" Trueman cried in a puny voice.

"Hold on, Trueman, I'll figure a way to get you out of there."

The field of sticks continued to shout, "Pick ME! I'm the knight! I'm Sir Taylor! I'm first knight to the king! Pick me and I'll treat you to a feast!"

"Caitlyn! Avry! Help me!" Emelia shouted. By the sound of her cry it could only mean one thing; she had joined Trueman and the army of ugly sticks. Her body became a decrepit, rotten, pimpled stick.

"I told you that your appetite would get you into trouble, Emelia," Caitlyn complained.

"Alright, let's think...all these ugly sticks are trying to make us believe that they are Sir Taylor, the knight. What question could we asked them that only Taylor would know?" Avry wondered.

"We should just ask them who gave him his sword," Emelia replied.

"Wow, Emelia, for someone who turned into an ugly stick, I guess you were paying attention," Caitlyn said with a chuckle.

"Okay, Caitlyn, you take the left side of the field and I'll take the right side of the field. Be careful and wait for the correct answer," Avry said as he turned and started walking toward the right. But no sooner did Avry start walking when he heard Caitlyn cry, apologetically, "Avry—I'm so sorry!"

Avry slowly turned around, trying not to fear the worst, only to see that Caitlyn, too, had been turned into a wretched ugly stick. "Caitlyn, I thought I told you to wait for the correct answer," he said with a huff.

"I did, Avry, honest—"

"Okay, which one of you sticks tricked my sister?!" Avry was livid.

"I did, sir," one of the ugly stick's said—the one closest to Caitlyn.

"Well, who are you, and how do you know the answer if you are not Sir Taylor, the knight?" Avry griped.

"My name is Arthur Miller; I am brother to the king of Epalushia, and best friend to Sir Taylor, the knight. So please don't be angry with your sister, she didn't know any better."

"Well, this is great, how am I to find Sir Taylor by myself in this huge field?"

"Well, I can tell you with one thing. I do know that Kildane hid Taylor in this field so that no one could find him," Arthur said.

"Great. That tells me a lot." Avry said sarcastically. "Okay, you guys, don't go anywhere, I'll be back."

"HA, HA, you are so funny, Avry," Trueman said as he cussed.

"Oops," Avry said as he shrugged. "Sorry about that, you guys, I forgot. Okay, I'll be right back." He chuckled and then began looking through the field and asking questions to other ugly sticks.

Avry searched for hours and talked with many of the sticks, but none of them seemed to know much about Sir Taylor. He stopped and asked another cursed piece of wood, "Excuse me, can you tell me if you know Sir Taylor, the knight?"

"Well, yes, he was helping us fight off the giants. I think he was somewhere behind me when I was running to save my horse from a giant. Then, of course, it happened. Just look at me, look at all of us!" the stick sobbed.

"Okay thanks," Avry said and he continued to ask question to other sticks. Finally, flustered and frustrated, he threw his hands into the air, shouting, "Does anyone know where Sir Taylor is?" His voice echoed in the ghost town.

A very tall, twisted stick yelled out—it sounded like a magnified shouting aluminum can, "I'm Sir Taylor...release me now...at once!"

"Prove it," Avry challenged bitterly.

"Well, I'm ordinarily a tall, dark, and handsome individual. I also have..."

"Stop," Avry said, holding out his hand, "just answer one question. Where did you get your sword?"

"Well, that's easy—um—you see...all great knights make their own swords, and..."

"Enough. You're a fake."

"I'm sorry. It's just that I can't stand being stuck here in the ground all the time," the ugly stick whined.

"I'm sorry for you, and for my brother and sisters. Somehow I'll find a way to break the curse. See ya, wouldn't want to be ya," Avry said, his sarcasm at its peak. All he could taste was the dry dirt that hung in the air. There was smell of brimstone, and something rumbled softly in the distance.

Avry moved through the field, closer to New Gander village. The village that was once made of stone and wood had mostly fallen and crumbled to the ground. Only a few desolate houses stood untouched by the giant's destruction.

The hot sun had made Avry dizzy and exhausted as he climbed through the ruins of New Gander. His eyes rolled back into his head, and he collapsed onto a large moss-covered boulder. He could barely focus on anything around him as he clung onto the cold, furry stone and held himself up. Suddenly a loud cracking sound came from inside the oversized rock. Avry's body vibrated as the stone began to split down the middle. Dust and debris flew into the air, while he stepped back, away from the boulder that had split into two pieces. Both halves crashed to the ground with a BOOM!

Avry paused for a minute, as the dust settled. He wobbled back and forth and wasn't quite sure if this was real or a dream. A shiny ugly stick emerged from the center of the split boulder.

The ugly stick coughed several times, and then began to speak, saying, "I beg your pardon, is there anyone there? It's not you is it, Kildane?"

"Hi, yes, well, that is, no, I am not Kildane and yes, there is someone here," Avry answered, approaching the ugly stick cautiously.

"Well, it's about time someone found me. I am very grateful, young sir, and forever in your debt."

"The name is Avry, and I haven't come this far to be fooled by some silly trick."

"Well, Sir Avry, I can assure you that there are no tricks here. Please pull me out of the ground and free me from this curse."

"What is your name?"

"Sir Taylor Frip, first knight to King Oliver, and protector of New Gander."

"I suppose anyone could know that. Where did you get your sword, Sir Taylor Frip?"

"I assure you that I am not lying. However, I received the sword from a wizard named Zita. The sword is strong and powerful and will kill any evil warlock."

"I will break you into a million pieces if you are lying," Avry said with a scowl. He stepped closer to the ugly stick, closed his eyes, slowly reached his trembling hand out, and grabbed firmly on the ugly stick. He pulled the stick out of the ground and felt a strong cold vibration reach up his arm. Avry quickly opened his eyes and gawked at the beautiful steel sword that he was holding in his hands.

"Ah, that is much better," Taylor took a deep breath.

Avry looked closely at the sword's shiny blade and saw the mirrored face of Sir Taylor, the knight. He swung the sword around in the air, stuck it under his belt, and then rushed back to where his siblings lay stuck in the ground—cursed and entombed in thin, twisted, decrepit strands of wood.

Chapter 12
Avry's Good Deed

"Where are we going, young chap?" Taylor asked.

"I've got to figure out a way to get my brother and sisters out of here and find and confront Kildane," Avry replied while he walked briskly through the field of ugly sticks. They winced, cried, and whined as he passed by, "Help us...Please!"

"Don't they ever shut up?" Avry griped, he held up the sword and looked at Sir Taylor's mirrored face. "Besides, I'm the one that could use some help here."

"Well, I think I can be of some assistance."

"Oh really, you are the one stuck inside a sword...how are you going to help me, Taylor? Huh? Go on...tell me."

The face in the sword frowned, "Well, I don't plan on being in here forever. You see, Kildane cast this spell on me, and I have been imprisoned in this sword for many years. Now that you have found me, all you have to do is use me for a good deed, and I will be released from this long cold blade of steel."

Avry began to walk faster and said, "I still don't see how you are going to help me release my brother and sisters from the ugly stick curse."

"Young man, we will take the ugly sticks to the unicorns and they will release the curse."

“Well, that sounds great, except for two things. First, I am going after Kildane, and second, how do I pick up the ugly sticks if I can’t touch them?”

“You can take the sticks out of the ground if you use this steel sword or something other than flesh.”

Avry stopped dead in his tracks. He quickly reached in his backpack and took out Captain Slaughter’s steel glove. The glove felt heavy and cold as Avry slipped it on his hand. He felt his nerves quiver like snakes running through his veins. Avry ran over to Trueman’s stick and pulled him out of the ground.

“Hi, Trueman, you’re going for a little ride,” Avry said happily, as he put the Trueman-stick in his backpack.

Avry hurried over to Emelia and Caitlyn’s ugly sticks and put them in his backpack as well.

“Look at me, I’m a stick!” Caitlyn shouted. She began to sob,

“I hope you learned your lesson, Trueman, you should have never touched that dragon egg.”

“Look at me, Caitlyn...I’m a stick too,” Trueman said in a squeaky voice.

“Yeah, and an ugly one at that,” Emelia said.

Avry held his hands up in a stopping gesture and said, “Calm down, guys. After I get Kildane, we are going to see the unicorns to release you from the curse.” He turned about face and headed toward the auburn hills.

The face in the sword frowned, saying, “I hope you are ready for a fight to the death. And please tell me why it is that you are going after Kildane."

"Listen, Sir Taylor, it's a long story. I'll explain it along the way to Kildane's cave."

Avry told Sir Taylor about their journey as he climbed the auburn hills. The grassy hill was very steep and hard to climb. Avry slipped backward several times while he climbed toward the top. He dropped to one knee, got up, and then dropped to his butt. Suddenly while Avry sat on the grassy hillside he spotted the dark figure that had been following them. Except this time the dark figure was climbing the hill ahead of them.

"Hey, maybe it's Kildane," Avry said, he held the sword up so Taylor could see. "No, that is not him...he's too short, and that is not something that he would wear."

"So, who is this person and what is he after?" Avry asked.

"Avry, run after him and find out why he's been following us," Caitlyn squeaked.

"Maybe its not us he's after, look!" Avry yelled.

"It's pirates!" Taylor cried.

Captain Slaughter landed his ship on top of the hill next to Kildane's cave. Avry ducked down behind a large bush and peered through the starlight map to get a better look. "Hey guys, it's Captain Slaughter, and he's fighting with Raider."

"Where's Kildane?" Trueman asked.

"I don't see him or the egg...Oh, wait, here he comes. He just came out of the cave holding the cane and the mushroom harp strings are still on it."

Raider darted into the cave while Kildane held up his magic cane and shot fireballs toward Captain Slaughter's ship. Captain Slaughter and his men climbed aboard the ship and began to take off.

"Hey, our mysterious follower is getting away on Slaughter's ship!" Avry shouted.

The dark figure clutched onto a rope that hung from the side of the pirate ship, and shimmied his way up to the ship. Slaughter's ship flew high into the clouds and then out of sight.

"Great, now we will never know who has been following us," Trueman squealed.

"Yeah, but Willow might find out," Avry said with a smirk.

Avry continued his struggle to climb to the top of the hill carrying everyone's heavy backpacks, the ugly sticks, and the heavy steel sword. Gusts of wind intensified as he approached the hilltop. He dropped to his stomach and crawled up the rest of the hillside.

When Avry finally reached the top, there was no sign of Kildane, Raider, or Captain Slaughter and the ship of pirates.

"Sir Avry, I think you should prepare yourself before you step foot into that cave..." Taylor warned.

"Why? How bad can it be in there?" Trueman squeaked.

"What do you care, Trueman, you're not the one going in there, I am," Avry said, swallowing hard and peering into the dark cave.

Before Trueman could say another word Sir Taylor continued, "Remember, you are not only entering a cave; you are entering the home of an evil warlock. This cave reeks with death, you'll feel like you are walking into hell, and if you're not careful it will eat you alive."

"Avry, don't take us in there, leave us out here!" Emelia shrieked.

"That's fine, you guys can wait out here, while I go inside by myself. But personally, I don't think it looks any better out here," he said, as he dropped the backpacks on the ground and brushed his hands together. He could smell his own fear. His hands were cold and clammy, and he felt his nerves spike through his skin.

Dark clouds swirled overhead in a circular motion; thunder and lighting crashed in the sky, and hail began to fall hard and fast to the ground.

"Well…I'm going in. You guys have fun out here," Avry said with a forced smile. He held the sword of the knight tight in his hand as he walked slowly toward the cave entrance. A rush of hot air blew back his long hair. The foul smell of brimstone, smoke, and sulfur made Avry's nose twinge.

Taylor's reflection looked into Avry's eyes, "Don't worry, Sir Avry. Just remember, you will strike fear into Kildane once he sees the sword. But his magic is evil, and his illusions could bring you down, so just be brave."

"Easier said then done, Sir Taylor. I wish I was back home hunting for burlybeasts rather than doing this."

"Avry, come back and get us! We want to come with you!" Caitlyn called out, but it was too late.

Avry had already entered the cave and could no longer hear his brother and sisters' cries.

Deep inside the cave, the walls burned bright with fire. The floor was covered with snakes of all sizes, and they slithered and hissed beneath Avry's feet. Rivers of hot burning lava flowed on each side of Avry, as he continued down a path that took him deeper inside the cave. The path was grim—the worst he had yet encountered.

He listened while a deep voice screamed fiercely from somewhere close by. He crept behind a large rock that spiked up from the ground and peered over it to see who was yelling. Kildane stood face to face with Raider. In one hand he held the dragon egg, and in the other he yanked the sea monkey's spiked orange hair. Raider shook from the warlock's blood-curdling screams, "If you let that bloody pirate interfere with this plan one more time, I'll make sure that you don't live another day!"

Raider escaped Kildane's grip and cowered in a corner. "Yes, Master Kildane, I won't let it happen again," he said with his knees knocking.

"Now take this egg to the giants' castle, get your gold, and leave for good," Kildane pointed to his right.

"Yes, master," Raider said and ducked into a small cave without another word.

Kildane held his gold cane toward where Raider exited; a bolt of lightening crashed into rocks, crumbling and sealing off the cave.

"Great, now how are we going to get Raider?" Avry whispered to Taylor.

"Avry, we will catch up to Raider later...let's get Kildane first."

A small, lumpy black rock was attached to a necklace around Kildane's neck, and he held it up to his eye. Avry could barely hear Kildane's muffled voice as he talked to himself from behind the dark black mask, saying, "Now let me see what those pesky Treelanders are doing."

"Look no further, Kildane! I'm here and I brought a friend," Avry said, standing tall and holding up the sword of the knight.

Kildane's eyes squinted from behind the mask, "Young man, you and that sword are no match for me. Leave now while you have the chance. You should have left well alone after our meeting at the faerie garden."

"You shouldn't be so quick to judge," Avry said, pointing the sword at his enemy. "This is no ordinary sword. Perhaps it's been too long since you've seen Sir Taylor, the first night to King Oliver."

"Impossible, that must be an imposter. The sword of the knight is cursed," the warlock said with a slight tremor in his voice.

"Enough talk, Kildane. You have something that I need, and I am not leaving without the harp strings."

Kildane waved his hand invitingly, saying, "Come and get them, boy."

Avry raised the sword over his head and charged at Kildane without a second thought. His father would have been proud if he had seen his courage and determination. Cold air rushed through the cave as Kildane waved his cane over a small chasm in the floor behind him. Hundreds of screeching ghost owls poured out of the ground and filled the cave. Avry's heart pounded hard and fast as the ghost owls picked him up and tossed him into a wall.

"Avry, just concentrate on Kildane and don't let his tricks scare you," Taylor coached.

Avry swung the sword at the ghost owls as they approached. They disappeared one by one, as the sword struck each one.

Kildane became furious and shot firebolts at Avry from his cane. Avry crouched behind the sword and was amazed when the bolts of fire bounced off the steel blade.

"Kildane!" Avry called out. "I told you this sword is the real deal. Now give me those strings!"

"You may have beaten my curse on the sword, but you cannot beat the power of my magic," Kildane said.

Kildane's cane began to glow and spin around in the air like a spinning wheel. The spinning cane spiraled through the air, clashed with the sword and sent Avry flying backward.

Avry's head was inches away from a stream of boiling lava; he slowly picked himself off the ground and charged at Kildane at full force.

Kildane's cane flew back into his hands as Avry approached him. He held the glowing cane in the air, and it collided with Avry's sword. Sparks exploded into the air like fireworks. Kildane's cane changed its form once again—it became an electrical sword. He struck down onto the sword of the knight over and over. Avry held the sword tightly while his hands burned and vibrated from Kildane's forceful blows.

After his repeated beating down on Avry, the warlock snapped his head back and howled, "Strike as hard as you want, you will not win. Sir Taylor could not beat me before and you cannot beat me now with his sword—you are too weak without your sisters and brother. Oh, and it's too bad about your precious mom and dad. I guess you could say they're stuck between a rock and a hard place." Avry became enraged at Kildane's hysterics, his face turned scarlet, and his lips peeled back into a snarl. He swung his sword continuously into Kildane's cane. The strikes became faster and harder and pushed Kildane further back into the cave, closer and closer toward the chasm in the floor.

Kildane jabbed his cane into Avry's stomach. Avry lost his breath and fell to the ground. Disoriented, he struggled to get up. His fingers clawed at the gritty floor.

Long, evil fingers slipped out of Kildane's robe and grabbed Avry around his neck. Blood began to trickle down Avry's chest.

Kildane picked the Treelander up by the throat with one hand and dangled Avry in front of him. Avry tried desperately to gasp for air while Kildane's hand squeezed tighter—the warlock's fingers penetrated the boy's flesh.

Avry could feel the sword slipping from his hand, he started to feel faint, and flashes of his family were running though his head.

Kildane began to laugh and shout. “Now you listen to me, you little Treelander. You’re not going to bother me or anyone else again. The dragon egg is mine and there’s nothing you can do about it.”

Avry reached within himself for every last ounce of energy. His vision was fading and he choked for oxygen. He could taste death on his tongue. Was this the dream-demon? Was this his vision, his nightmare? He wasn’t sure, but he knew for certain that the sword felt like an elephant in his hand. He thought he heard his brother and sisters screaming, “Strike now Avry, strike now!” He opened his eyes and looked into the face of his enemy. He reached back and swung the sword with every last bit of strength. The sword sliced Kildane’s arm clean off at the elbow.

Kildane’s arm immediately turned to dust and the cane dropped to the ground. The warlock fell backward and out of sight into the dark black chasm in the cave floor. For a moment, a blinding flash of violet light filled the cave.

Avry crawled slowly over to the evil warlock’s cane and pulled off the harp strings.

“Good show, Avry. You’ve defeated Kildane once and for all,” Taylor cheered.

Avry looked into the sword and noticed that the reflection of Sir Taylor had vanished. He looked puzzled as he inspected both sides of the sword.

“Sir Taylor, are you in there? Where are you?”

“Right here, Sir Avry, live and in the flesh.”

Avry spun around and saw a knight dressed in shining silver armor. Taylor held out his hand in gratitude, "Thank you, Avry, for your good deed has released me from my prison. And in return, I will stay with you and help you get the dragon egg back."

Avry clutched his side as he regained his breath, saying, "Great, we could use your help. But first we need to return these strings to the fairies. Let's go show the others."

Avry and Taylor moved quickly out of the evil cave that slithered with horror and death. The briliant light from the sun pushed its way into the cave as they approached the exit. Outside, the rain had stopped. Trueman, Caitlyn, and Emelia were still bickering about the fact that they were ugly sticks.

"Avry just left us here, how could he do this?" Caitlyn said.

"I'm hungry. What do you suppose an ugly stick eats?" Emelia asked.

"That rain left me waterlogged," Trueman whined.

Avry stepped outside of the cave, cleared his throat, and said, "Et-hem! Did you guys miss me?" He stood with his new friend by his side.

"Avry, you made it back!" Trueman cheered.

"Yes, and I've got the strings. Now who has the faerie dust?" Avry asked and then shook his head.

"It's in my backpack," Caitlyn said.

Avry reached inside Caitlyn's backpack and pulled out a handful of faerie dust. He sprinkled the flakey gold dust onto the magical harp strings and stood back. The Treelanders and Sir Taylor vanished immediately into a big puff of smoke and were transported back to the faerie garden.

The warlock was defeated, and now it was time for the Treelanders to put the pieces back together. To rescue Willow, cure the ugly sticks, save the dragon egg, and get the giants' swamp water. A little more than what they bargained for when the first left on their journey. However, their will and determination was stronger than ever.

Chapter 13
Willow's Surprise

To travel from the auburn hills to the faerie garden would normally take a half day on foot; however, the magical transportation took the Treelanders and Sir Taylor less than a second to make their journey—just a blink of an eye and they had returned.

When the Treelanders arrived back at the faerie garden, the magical strings flew out of Avry's hands and reattached onto the mushroom harp.

Fairies flew merrily and danced around the Treelanders and Sir Taylor. The magical music of the mushroom harp played once again.

Nire flew over to Avry who was holding the backpack full of ugly sticks, and said, "Ooh, the ugly stick curse. We haven't been able to find a cure for that one."

"Ah, yes, young lady. It is only the magical sound of a unicorn's horn that will cure this curse," Taylor said knowingly.

Krista flew around Sir Taylor and said curiously, "How is it that a knight would know about the cure to an evil spell?"

Taylor stood up and said proudly, "My spell was a double spell. I guess old Kildane thought it would drive me mad if I knew the cure, and couldn't do anything about it while I was imprisoned in the sword."

Ali sat on top of the mushroom harp scratching her head, "What about Kildane, is he d-d-dead?"

Avry pushed back his hair exposing his scratched neck and said, "Yeah, I chopped off his arm and then he fell into a bottomless pit. I really thought I was a goner."

"Well, this gives us reason to celebrate," Nire said as she flew about.

But Avry shook his head, saying, "Time is running out. I'm sure Raider has probably given the egg to the giants by now."

Krista hovered in front of Avry's face and said, "It is almost nightfall. Raider is too lazy to travel by night. You should reconsider."

"But we need to get to the unicorns to free my brother and sisters from the ugly stick curse," Avry said.

Taylor rubbed his stomach and said, "Avry, we will leave tonight when the thirteenth moon is at its highest peak in the sky, but for now let's enjoy a feast. It's been too long since I've had a meal. Please don't deny a hungry man who has been imprisoned for years."

The air was filled with the aroma of warm apple pie, honey- roasted burlybeast, blueberry juice, and chocolate-covered cinnamon sticks. Bright, cheerful melodies continued to play from the mushroom harp as everyone joined in the feast. The faerie garden had never been so joyful and full of excitement.

Avry, Taylor, and the ugly sticks sat next to a small campfire that burned brightly.

"This is so not fair! All this great food, and I

can't even eat it," Emelia whined.

"Here Emelia, try some blueberry juice," Avry poured blueberry juice out of his cup onto Emelia's ugly stick.

"Very funny, Avry," Emelia cussed.

Taylor bit into a roasted burlybeast leg and then said, "Yes, it is a funny thing about an ugly stick. You are never hungry and you cannot drink or eat. What an evil curse."

The faeries continued to dance and celebrate around the campfire until the flames burned low. Avry and Taylor said goodnight to the faeries as they took to the branches of the weeping willow tree.

Nire turned around and quickly flew back over to Avry, saying, "I'll be back to help you guys when the thirteenth moon is at its peak."

"Right," Taylor said with a wink of an eye.

Nire dashed off with the rest of the faeries, and Avry stared at Taylor—confused and somewhat annoyed.

"What was that about, all the winking and stuff?" Avry griped.

"In good time, Sir Avry, in good time." Taylor yawned as he layed back and shut his eyes.

Avry just shook his head and layed down to rest as well. The night had become completely silent; even the mushroom harp could barely be heard. Avry stared up at the stars that shone brightly and watched the trees as they swayed softly back and forth.

"You don't think I'm sleeping, do you, brother?" Trueman asked wisely.

"Boy, Trueman, you made me jump out of my skin!" Avry almost shouted.

"Oh yeah, that's the other thing about ugly sticks—they don't sleep either," Taylor said with one eye open.

"Great," Avry rolled his eyes and winced as he felt his neck—the welted scratches made it almost impossible to fall asleep.

"Taylor, what is to become of the people of New Gander? Can we cure them?" Caitlyn asked.

"We've just got to convince the unicorns that it is safe to return to Epalushia, and then I am sure they will cure everyone of the ugly stick curse."

"Well, I'm sure that once they find out Kildane is dead, they will come, won't they?" Trueman asked.

"I'm sure they'll be happy for that," Taylor replied.

The Treelanders continued to ask Sir Taylor about his adventures as a knight. Caitlyn, on the other hand, was more interested in a good love story, and asked, "What about Arthur and Queen Sheena, do you think that...?"

"No, I don't care to discuss that love war," Taylor barked. Taylor took to his feet and began to pace back and forth.

"I'm sorry if I said something wrong," Caitlyn said apologetically.

"Let's just change the subject, okay young lady-stick?" Taylor demanded. He sat back down next to Avry and stared into the campfire.

"So tell me, Sir Taylor, did you ever run into Captain Slaughter?" Trueman asked.

"No, he arrived in Epalushia after the ugly stick curse."

"Well, he's going to leave after we get Willow back safely," Avry grumbled.

"That's if we can catch him. He never sits still for too long," Emelia complained.

"I hope Willow is okay...I really miss her," Caitlyn squeaked.

"I'm sure she's fine. I don't think those pirates knew what they were bargaining for when they captured her," Avry's snicker turned into a yawn.

Willow had been fine, for in fact she had become a hassle for the pirates to deal with over the past few days, fighting with them about everything to get her way, and on board Captain Slaughter's ship they were all in for another big surprise.

Captain Slaughter had guided his ship to the giant's swamp in hope of finding Raider and the egg. Everyone on board was sound asleep; even Slug and Willy (who were supposed to be on Willow's nighttime watch) had passed out.

A mysterious and uninvited guest lurked in the darkness and slithered about the ship. The mysterious dark figure that had been following the Treelanders along their journey had now crept into the room where Willow was asleep.

An empty bottle of rum fell out of Willy's hand onto the floor and startled the mysterious guest, only for a minute, but he realized quickly that the pirates were intoxicated with rum.

The dark figure removed his hood and exposed the bold face of a handsome young man with blue eyes and short blonde hair. He carefully crawled over to Willow, put his hand over her mouth, and shook her gently.

"Willow...wake up," the mysterious man whispered.

The moonlight cast shadows on the walls and objects in the room. Willow's heart was pounding with fear as she woke only to hear her screams silenced by the hand of the mysterious figure crouching over her. Her eyes opened wider as she got her first glimpse of the mysterious man's familiar face.

"Prince William! What are you doing here?" Willow shouted.

"Shhh, you'll wake all these scoundrels, and then we'll both be captured," Prince William said.

Prince William untied Willow's hands and feet. Willow stared at him in amazement and could hardly talk, muttering, "I-I don't understand..."

"I have been following your path since you left Sky Lake."

"I knew I wasn't losing my mind. Everyone just kept telling me that I was seeing things."

"You weren't, I just didn't want to be seen by the pirates, so I kept myself hidden and out of sight."

"But why did you leave the castle?" Willow asked.

"Strange things have been happening at the castle lately. I've been trying to figure out what has been going on. Mom and Dad have been acting quite peculiar, and then the other night I saw something."

"What was it?" Willow whispered and rubbed her sore wrists.

"I think my Dad's life is in danger. I saw a man enter the throne room; he was all dressed in black and wore a mask. I could hear yelling and thrashing about, and then the man dressed in black ran off quickly toward your village."

"Well, I still don't understand why you are so worried about us," Willow said. "After all, you are royalty and we are just Treelanders."

"I heard the man—who ever he was—say that he wished to kill everyone...even the Treelanders. I just thought you should know and..." his voice trailed off as his face went pink.

"And what?" Willow asked curiously.

Prince William pulled at his hair and scrunched his face, saying, "I was worried about Caitlyn. I have fallen in love with her and...I wanted to come help you find the egg. I was afraid that I would never see her again."

"Oh, brother, you need to put this love thing on hold, and we need to get out of here, like now!"

Willow and Prince William slipped into a large storage cabinet and began to devise a plan—a plan to defeat Captain Slaughter and his men once and for all. Willow thought it sounded like the best plan to date.

The thirteenth moon of Epalushia had reached its highest peak, and it illuminated the land in a light blue glow. Meanwhile, back at the faerie garden, someone else was about to be surprised by a familiar face.

Beams of light showered the sleeping land of faeries. Nire was aware that she had only minutes to get Avry and Taylor on their way or it would be too late. The faerie zoomed down to Avry and Taylor and shook them abruptly, saying, "Avry, Taylor, you must wake up quickly."

"I think I slept for about a minute, what about you, Sir Taylor," Avry said rubbing his eyes.

"You'll be just fine, lad, now let's get moving. Don't want to keep those unicorns waiting, do you?"

"Why? Do they know we're coming?" Avry asked.

"Well...no, but I'm sure they could use a little company," Taylor replied.

Nire lead them over to the pond that slept beneath the weeping willow tree. Tassels fluttered through the air as Nire waved her white magic wand at a large lily pad in the middle of the pond. "It's time to go," she said pointing to the center of the murky water.

Beams of silver light flowed from Nire's magic wand and connected with the lily pad. The beam pulled the pad like a fish on a string and it floated over to the pond's edge.

Sir Taylor climbed aboard the wet, green carpet while Avry looked on in disbelief, "We're going to travel on that thing?" he yelled.

"Have a little faith, Avry. Now get on quick!" Taylor said. "Don't worry. I've traveled like this before. It's perfectly safe."

Avry carted the heavy backpacks containing the ugly sticks, and his siblings' supplies. He thought his legs were weakening. His entire body ached and his neck was on fire from where Kildane had grabbed him. He had barely gotten himself on the lily pad when it started to levitate into the night sky.

Small green arms and hands grew out of the lily pad and fastened onto the passengers. Without warning, the green pad took off like a streak of light. Higher into the sky, up to the stars, they traveled as the thirteenth moon of Epalushia grew near. Avry tried to speak but the speed was too fast to utter a word. Wonderful clusters of stars flashed by them as the lily pad dodged and darted through space.

Like a magnet, the green flying carpet was being lured into the gigantic purple moon. Thick clouds of purple haze surrounded them during their approach on the moon's surface. With a BUMP and a THUMP, the wild space ride came to an abrupt halt. The lily pad wobbled back and forth and then floated gently onto a small thick, grassy field.

Heavy rain covered the land. It had been almost impossible to see. A thin layer of fog hovered over the dark and gloomy land. A desolate land, that didn't appear at all inviting or even hopeful for the Treelanders. Avry's heart hurt; he felt a sudden sadness overwhelm him. He had thought for a moment he was going to be ill, but maintained. But what was in store for him and his family was still uncertain.

Chapter 14
Double Vision

Avry and Sir Taylor stepped off the lily pad and their feet sank into the marshy surface. The water level was over their ankles, and the temperature was lukewarm. It was perhaps the first warm bath that their feet had had in days.

"Where are we?" Avry said sleepily.

"I haven't the foggiest...this doesn't seem right," Taylor replied. "We must have made a wrong turn somewhere—"

"Look—over there, it looks like a horse, I think," Avry said, as his heart beat rapidly.

Avry and Taylor trudged through the soggy wet grass and mud. They began to pick up the pace as a white stallion came into clear view. The white horse grazed in the marshy field contently. A foul smell of mold and mildew filled the air with each step that Avry took. He thought again about being sick as he gagged on the still air.

The stallion raised its white fluffy mane and stared deep into the eyes of the newcomers. Upon the stallions nose was a silver liquid spot that swirled around in a circular motion and picked up speed when he spoke. "Are you here to help?" the stallion asked. "Our beautiful land has been destroyed, and each day gets sadder than the last."

"We were hoping you could help us...look," Taylor said, pointing to the backpack full of ugly sticks. The stallion quickly turned its head and began to trot away.

"Wait...maybe we could help each other," Avry called.

The stallion was so disappointed that he didn't even stop; he just continued to trot out of sight.

Taylor gave the Treelander a reassuring pat on the shoulder, saying, "Don't worry, Avry...it's the unicorns that we need to find anyway. Let's keep moving."

"This is the most depressing land. I feel so nauseous," Emelia cried out. "But how can that be?"

"I believe that I'm getting waterlogged," Caitlyn cried.

"Hurry up, Avry, I don't want to be a stick any longer, and besides I can't stand Caitlyn's crying anymore," Trueman said desperately.

Avry felt like grabbing the sticks, shaking them, and saying, "Guys! Relax. As soon as we see a unicorn, you will all be back to normal. I promise."

Avry and Taylor walked deeper into the dark, wet, and gloomy land. Purple haze hung low to the ground, fir trees surrounded them on each side, and rain poured in bucketfuls. There had been no sign of unicorns or any other animals for that matter.

Sir Taylor stopped short when he heard a faint sound of voices— the voices came from within the fog and directly in front of them. The fog was so dense that Avry lost site of Taylor who was walking right beside him.

"Taylor, is that you talking?" Avry asked. "Where are you?"

"To your left…and, no, it's not me talking. I think we should prepare ourselves. There is something close by and heading this way."

A low rumble shook the ground while loud piercing shrieks filled the airwaves. The thumping sounds of hooves grew louder and seemed to surround Avry and Taylor from all sides. The fog had cleared for a moment, revealing a herd of wild horses.

Darkness closed in on Avry and Taylor when the herd of horses moved in for a closer look. Hooves pranced on the marshy surface and splashed puddles of mud onto the unwelcome visitors.

Taylor drew out his sword while Avry threw down the backpacks and fumbled for Trueman and Caitlyn's swords. They were completely surrounded by the angry mob. The horses snorted and grunted loudly. Trueman began screaming from behind Avry's head, "Avry, do something!"

"I don't understand...where are all the unicorns?" Avry said, as his head snapped from side to side. He tried to back up, but it was pointless.

"It looks as if perhaps this lynch mob wiped them off the planet," Taylor said as he spun his sword in the air and moved back to back with Avry.

Suddenly, the herd silenced and bowed their heads. The circle of horses parted, revealing two new guests. The newcomers slowly pranced through the mud. Avry's eyes opened wide when the two purple stallions appeared out of the fog; he took a few steps backward, and his mouth dropped open, in awe of the breathtaking sight.

With each step closer it became more apparent that the two horses shared one thing in common. The large purple steed had upon it two heads that were identical in size and shape. The two- headed creature stopped only inches from Avry's face. Its warm breath hit the cold, damp air and fogged Avry's vision. He froze in place as the steeds began to speak to him in unison, "Why have you come here and what do you seek?"

"We are looking for the unicorns to free my brother and sisters of the ugly stick curse. Do you know of this curse?" Avry asked.

"Look no further, for you will get no such wish today," the two- headed steed said grimly.

"What do you mean?" Taylor cried and waved his sword. "What have you done with the unicorns?"

Silver spots began to swirl like pools of mercury on the horse's noses.

"We are the unicorns that you seek. We have just been robbed of our beautiful magical horns," the two-headed unicorn said in a droning voice.

"Who would do such a thing?" Caitlyn asked. Her voice was so squeaky and faint.

From out of the herd, a yellow-striped unicorn charged Avry down to the ground. The unicorn stood over Avry's body growling and snorting as he sniffed Avry's backpack that contained Captain Slaughter's glove.

"Where did you get this?" the unicorn said as he clutched the black glove in his teeth.

The two-headed unicorn brushed the yellow-stripe backward, saying, "Back up, Yazzo, this boy doesn't look dangerous."

Avry nodded, swallowed hard, and said, "I-I'm not. That glove belongs to Captain Slaughter, a rotten awful pirate that has captured my sister Willow. I got the glove during a fight and kept it."

Yazzo spat the glove to the ground, and said, "This was the glove that took our horns and caused us great pain. It's been raining, and this land has been depressing, ever since."

The hornless two-headed unicorn pulled Avry to his feet and said, "My name is Tueen, the only unicorn that can cure the ugly stick curse. But without my horns I'm afraid I have no healing magic."

"Why would Captain Slaughter steel your horns? I mean what good are they to him?" Emelia asked.

Tueen whined, "Kildane was behind it all. He tricked Slaughter into steeling the horns in exchange for a large golden treasure."

"Yeah, but Kildane didn't hold up his end of the bargain," Yazzo snapped. "He just made sure that the ugly stick curse could never be cured."

"That's what they must have been fighting about outside Kildane's cave," Trueman squeaked. "It was the dragon egg! Kildane never held up his end of the bargain by giving up the egg to Captain Slaughter."

Avry smiled and gazed at the Trueman-stick; he felt happy at his brother's conclusion but then saddened by the appearance of the cursed ugly stick.

"So the horns must still be on Captain

Slaughter's ship," Avry said.

Tueen looked around at her family of unicorns, shook her heads in agreement, and replied, "I think perhaps you could be right."

"All the more reason why we must find Captain Slaughter," Sir Taylor said.

"Yazzo and I can take you to the giant swamp where Slaughter and his men usually hang out," Tueen said.

Yazzo and Tueen stayed, while the herd of unicorns quickly dispersed and ran off into the rain and mist.

"Climb on, quickly," Yazzo said. He seemed forgiving.

Taylor and Avry climbed on the unicorns' soggy, wet backs. Avry clutched tightly onto the bag containing the ugly sticks as Tueen began to gallop into the darkness. They strode faster and more rapidly though the wet, grassy fields. Hard rain poured down and felt like pounding rocks on their faces, as the unicorns dashed faster. The loud, thudding hooves suddenly silenced as they lifted into the air, through the purple clouds, out of the dark gloomy land, and into the bright, beautiful stars and space. Colorful planets and stars blazed passed them, while the unicorns darted toward Epalushia. A globe of light illuminated the travelers—an imaginary globe. Avry would later say that he could not recall the trip.

The familiar planet of home grew closer into view, as the unicorns soared through the sky. The small island in the sky looked inviting compared to the gloomy planet of the unicorns. The travelers quickly approached a part of the forbidden land that they had yet to explore. Bright morning sun reflected off the ocean surface, while the unicorns flew over it just barely skimming the water.

The strong scent of salt, sand, and seaweed filled the ocean air. Taylor began to laugh with joy when he saw two dolphins swimming side by side and jumping in the air beside him. Avry looked around with a wide smile and amazement at the rich, beautiful land. The sound of the whispering wind intensified, and the unicorns charged even faster toward a small opening in the dark green jungle ahead. They floated over a small, twisting river that cut through the thick, plush woods. Birds chirped and whistled loudly as they passed by. Strange insects hummed and fluttered about, adding to the melody of the jungle critters. They finally arrived in the middle of the jungle where the eerie but inviting giants' swamp stood.

Moss-covered trees with long fur vines were settled throughout the swamp's edges. Green algae sat upon the thick and murky water that bubbled every so often in random spots.

Avry could hardly wait to get the swamp water that was needed to cure the fire and ice curse; he jumped off Tueen's back before she had a chance to land. A flock of pelicans scattered about as Avry landed with a *splash* in the marsh.

"Guys, we finally made it! The giants' swamp water, it's here, we're here!" Avry cheered in triumph as he splashed in the murky water.

"Quick, Avry, fill up the bottle!" Caitlyn cried.

Avry climbed to the edge of the swamp and sat down. He scurried through his backpack to find the bottle. He took out the witch's old brown potion bottle and pulled off the cork with a loud pop.

"How much do you think we'll need?" Trueman asked.

"I don't know," Avry exclaimed. "I'm just going to fill the whole thing up," he said with the biggest grin. He could hardly contain his excitement and kicked his feet in the air.

Avry carefully replaced the cork and sealed the swamp-filled bottle. He smiled and tucked it safely in his backpack.

"Job well done, Sir Avry," Sir Taylor said, as he and Yazzo approached.

"Hey, where's Captain Slaughter's ship?" Avry asked.

"The pain on my nose tells me that he is not too far from here," Yazzo whined.

"Yeah, but the question is where," Trueman squeaked. "He's so sneaky that we never seem to find him."

"Wait a minute...I'll use the starlight map," Avry said as he reached his hand into the sopping wet backpack and pulled out the soggy map. Water and mud dripped from the map when Avry brought it up to his eye.

Nothing happened.

No beam of light.

No super-powered vision.

There was a slight hesitation in Avry's voice as

the map drooped downward, and he said, "I—I think I better let this dry up." He cleared his throat and wiped the soggy parchment on his arm.

"Hey, the map worked in the coral caves, wonder why not here," Caitlyn said curiously.

"Great! Now we'll never find Slaughter," Emelia moaned. "I don't know how much more I can take of being an ugly stick."

The excitement of the giant swamp water and the whereabouts of Captain Slaughter had their emotions twisted in a knot. They all sat quietly and looked around at the strange jungle that oozed with humidity and jolted with uncommon noises.

Could it have been that Captain Slaughter was too swift and cunning for them? The Treelanders would like to think not. However, they would soon come to find out that Captain Slaughter was, in fact, closer than they thought.

Chapter 15
Willow's Revenge

The tall, sleek pirate ship was hidden safely on the far side of the giants' swamp, its sails camouflaged under green bushy trees and moss-covered vines. Slaughter's filthy crew was scattered about the ship, still in a deep sleep.

Willow and Prince William snuck quietly around the pirate ship and executed their escape plan. First, Prince William had plugged all the cannons so they would backfire, while Willow tied rope around Willy, Slug, and the rest of the pirates. Captain Slaughter, however, was safely locked and sleeping in his private cabin.

Willow gathered all the swords and pistols, while Prince William set a booby trap outside Captain Slaughter's cabin room door.

"Willow, I'm going below to disable the flying and submerging gears," the Prince whispered. "You stay up here and stand guard." He gave her a wink. Willow nodded her head, while he opened the hatch door and went down into the engine room.

With the prince out of sight, Willow leaned over the bow of the ship and threw all the swords and pistol into the murky swamp. They plopped and fizzed in the gooey water. "Yuck!" she said as she winced.

Meanwhile, down in the engine room, Prince William slithered passed a pirate that was sound asleep in his chair. Captain Slaughter would have been furious if he knew that his best guards were sleeping at that very moment. Sleeping was an understatement; they were dead to the sea from an overindulgence of Slug's homemade rum.

Prince William rubbed his nose at the musty-smelling room. He moved stealthily and gently pulled two glasslike tubes out of the ship's engine. The tubes were glowing red and made a soft humming sound. He put the tubes gently under his right arm and started to climb back up on deck. The ladder gave a sudden jerk and one of the tubes slipped and fell to the floor with a SMASH. The red neon tube let out a piercing whistle that was loud enough to wake anyone for miles around.

Willow and Prince William covered their ears in pain.

"Can't you stop that?" Willow shouted.

"I have no idea what you are saying," Prince William replied, climbing back on deck.

Captain Slaughter's door slammed open instantly. Willow looked on helplessly as he took one step out his door. He slid across the oil- greased wooden deck, smashed into two barrels full of water, and landed on his back.

Slaughter watched in disbelief as a large net fell on him and trapped him like a wild animal. He thrashed around inside the gnarled netting only to stop briefly to look at Willow through the holes in the twisted ropes.

"Argg! Who did this to me?!" Slaughter shouted, and then noticed Willow shaking. "You best be running, little lady, because I'm coming after you!"

"Not if I can help it!" Prince William roared.

"Slug, get me outta here, quick, or you'll be walking the plank!" Slaughter commanded.

Slug managed to get his hands free and reached down for his sword. His face went blank when he pulled out a bright yellow banana. Willow let out a huge laugh and then charged at Slug. With one blow to the knees, she knocked the pirate down into the engine room.

"Fire up the engines, Pepper, and take her down," Captain Slaughter yelled from underneath the net. "Nobody's getting off my ship, and that's an order!"

Pepper, the engine room pirate, turned a crank on the engine—without warning, a huge explosion smashed the engine into pieces. Smoke and fire began to billow out of the engine room door. Thick, deathly smoke suffocated all who stood in its way.

Back across the lake the ruckus didn't go without notice. Avry continued to dry off the map while the others snapped their necks toward the explosion. A bright plume of glowing orange spread across the sky. The eerie mass sent shivers up Avry's spine.

"What was that?" Trueman shouted. His little squeaky stick voice shrilled in horror.

"What sound would that be exactly? The whistle, the bang, or the shaking behind the trees," Avry said matter-of-factly.

"Look, beyond those trees, something is on fire!" Yazzo yelled and nodded across the swamp.

Black smoke drifted through the air and swept across the swamp. Air bubbles emerged rapidly from the thick, gloomy water. Leaves on the trees continued to shake from behind Avry and Taylor.

Taylor drew his weapon, and said, “Prepare yourself…something or someone is coming this way.”

Deep in the woods, loud footsteps could be heard splashing through the marsh. Avry’s heart pounded with every second of uncertainty that went by. Thoughts ran through his head, like “*Are the giants coming? What will I do when I see them? Am I prepared for this fight?*” Cold chills ran through his blood, as the footsteps grew louder.

The multitude of tree branches and twigs that snapped in the woods became overwhelming like the wild thunderstorms that occasionally rip through Treeland on hot summer nights.

Avry took a deep breath and let out a sigh—a heavy sigh, a fearful sigh that Taylor didn’t leave unnoticed. The brave knight reached over and placed his hand on Avry’s shoulder. Sir Taylor looked Avry straight in the eyes, and said, “Whatever happens, you must stand your ground. It’s a sign of bravery, and it will let your enemy know that you are not going down without a good fight.”

“G-g-got it, no problem,” Avry said, with a large swallow.

“Don’t worry, Avry, we are behind you all the way,” Emelia said.

“Very funny,” Avry said with a forced smile. “Thanks anyway.”

A large white sail peaked out from the billowing

smoke across the swamp. As each second passed, it became more evident to everyone whose ship was on fire.

"Look, it's Slaughter's ship!" Avry exclaimed, pointing to his left.

"Yazzo and I will deal with Slaughter. It looks like you already have company," Tueen said as she nodded both heads toward the woods.

The two-headed unicorn took off into the air and dashed toward the pirate ship. Yazzo follow behind her.

Avry and Taylor turned in a flash to see who had been rustling though the trees. Standing only a few feet away, were the strangest and fiercest creatures that Avry had ever laid eyes on.

"Trottles!" Taylor shouted.

Avry scowled and shrugged his shoulders, begging, "Taylor, can you please speak in a language that I can understand."

"Trottles," Taylor repeated. "Kildane's evil creation of trolls and sea turtles. They are vicious creatures. They will eat you whole if they have a chance."

Green snakelike skin covered the trottles' bodies; they had pointed beaks and long, spiked teeth; their heads looked like they were made of stone with two black, lifeless eyes like a shark. The trottles wore a hard shell that covered their body. They carried large spears in their claws and stomped them on the ground like beating a drum. The vulgar creatures gargled on phlegm in their throats as they approached Avry and Taylor.

A foul smell of burned hair wafted passed Avry's nose. "They smell awful!" he gagged.

"It's the tar that gives them that dreadful smell," Taylor said, almost choking.

"What tar?"

"The trottles live in tar pits under the swamp," Taylor replied, and he took a deep breath.

"I guess that would explain the ever-expanding army of trottles that just emerged from the swamp."

"Yep, that would do it."

Taylor swung his prized sword backward and then slashed it forward into a nearby trottle, splitting the mutant's armored shell down the middle, "Aha! They are no match for my sword!" Taylor let out a loud roar.

Avry began slicing at the trottles' shells with Trueman's sword. The sword did not have the same affect as Taylor's did. He tried using Caitlyn's sword—it was better, but not good enough. Both weapons had the same result—they bounced off the Trottles' shells and vibrated in Avry's sweaty palms.

The trottles snapped their sharp, pointed beaks. They clapped open and shut like two rocks smacking together. The creatures approached Avry; they were fearless and angered by Avry's attempted to harm them.

"It's okay Avry, just go for their legs!" Taylor shouted while he took down two trottles with one blow of his sword.

Avry and Taylor continued to battle the trottles, as they grew in numbers. They held their ground and fought vigorously. It appeared, however, that their efforts were coming to an end.

On the opposite side of the swamp, Willow and Prince William were heavily engaged in battle. The dirty-fighting pirates fought to regain their ship. Chaos encircled the swamp, and the trottles began to emerge around Captain Slaughter's ship.

A huge water fountain shot up from inside the engine room, the explosion from the engine blew a hole in the ship's floor ten feet wide.

On the main deck Prince William had a pirate clutched in his hands and flung him overboard. From the side of the ship came a loud scream, and then silence as a trottle pulled the pirate under the swamp. The water bubbled and fizzed around the struggling pirate. With one tug, the pirate had vanished.

Willow punched a one-eyed pirate in the face, while he tried desperately to untie his hands; she wasted no time and pushed the pirate overboard into the clutches of another trottle.

Slaughter's ship splintered into bits and continued to sink deeper while Slug wrestled to get Captain Slaughter free from the net; the fat-bellied pirate slipped and fell repeatedly onto the greasy floor, and became stained with black goop from head to toe.

"Slug, stop fooling around and get me out of here!"

Slaughter shouted.

Tueen and Yazzo made their approach and landed on the ship's deck, while Willow and Prince William just stared with open mouths.

"We are here to help you. Your brother, Avry, is here too," Tueen said.

"Avry's here?" Willow's eyes welled up with tears of joy.

"Alright, you pesky rats," Captain Slaughter snarled behind them. He looked flustered and out of breath, his hat was crinkled, and his hair looked like a rat's nest. He squinted into the eyes of his enemies and said, "My ship maybe sinking but you will walk the plank before I'm done with you."

"Not today, Slaughter," Prince William shouted and raised his sword.

Slaughter raised his sword and clashed hard with the Prince's mighty weapon. The steel blades screeched as they slid against each other.

Willow pushed a wooden barrel on its side and rolled it toward Slug, knocking him backward into the captain's cabin.

"Willow! No! What are you doing?" Prince William screamed.

Willow charged into the cabin room after the huge bald pirate without a reply.

Tueen flew over and kicked Slaughter in the back of the head, while Yazzo tried to get through the small cabin door. The yellow- striped unicorn began to smash the door frame with his hooves. He wrestled to get inside when he heard Willow scream in terror.

Willow entered the cabin room with a scowled face, "Where are you, you big ugly pirate?" Her eye's quickly spun around the room; she let out a blood-curdling scream and gasped for air—

Slug had swung down from the ceiling and kicked her clear to the opposite side of the room. Willow tried desperately to regain focus. Her sword slipped out of her hand and slid across the wooden floor. Flames crawled up the walls from the engine room below, as she struggled to find her weapon. Beads of sweat poured down her face from the blazing fire. Finally, from the corner of her eyes, she saw a rope that hung across the room. Dangling from the rope were colorful, pointed, funneled sticks. She reached up and pulled it down.

The large pirate closed in on Willow, and growled, "Come here, missy. No more biting or spitting at Slug today."

Willow flung the spike-covered rope around Slug's neck and fell back down onto the floor. Slug was inches from grabbing Willow when he felt a sudden tug backward.

"Young lady, run out of here!" Yazzo cried.

Willow crawled under Slug's legs as Yazzo pulled tighter on the rope. Slug's face turned blue, and he opened his mouth for air—air that never came. Yazzo quickly pulled Slug out of the ship and tossed him to the trottles that waited in the swamp below.

"Yazzo, you found our horns!" Tueen exclaimed.

Captain Slaughter had hung the beautiful unicorn horns like a trophy in his cabin. Yazzo became enraged at the thought of it.

Fire and smoke poured onto the main deck from Captain Slaughter's cabin door like a raging black river. It pooled around the captain and the prince. Captain Slaughter had the cold steel blade of his sword on Prince William's neck, and his scaly flush face was snarled as he said, "Say good-bye to your friends, prissy boy!"

Prince William pushed back with all his might, gritting his teeth, his face red. Slaughter's blade pushed on his skin deeper, almost penetrating into his veins. A slow trickle of blood ran down the prince's neck. "Don't call me pris..." his voice trailed off, and he began to gag.

Slaughter snapped his head back and laughed while he pushed his blade with no remorse. The prince felt the blade suddenly release, as something magically tugged Slaughter backward—

"What is happening?" The prince wondered as he rubbed his eyes. *"How could it be?"* Prince William looked on, befuddled.

Slaughter's body lifted into the air. He felt a sharp pain in the middle if his back, while he was pushed toward his burning cabin room. The captain looked down to his stomach—the tip of a horn had penetrated through him. He gasped in pain, and his eyes rolled back exposing the whites. Yazzo had got his horn back and drove Captain Slaughter into the raging inferno of the cabin room. A loud explosion blew the top of the captain's cabin sky high, sending wood, debris, and burning ash raining downward. That was the last time the Treelanders ever saw the likes of Captain Slaughter and the brave, yellow-striped unicorn named Yazzo.

Tueen grabbed the rope of unicorn horns and rushed into the air with Willow and Prince William riding on her large purple back. The pirate ship continued to crumble and burn into pieces; the remains sank into its dark grave at the bottom of the giant swamp.

The two-headed unicorn flew higher into the air and circled over to where Avry and Taylor were completely surrounded by trottles.

Willow cupped her hands around her mouth and shouted, "Avry, up here! It's Willow. I'm here at last!"

Avry heard Willow's voice and then fainted when a trottle grabbed him in its clutches. Taylor struggled to get free from two trottles that held him tightly. The ugly mutants quickly disappeared into the jungle with Avry, Taylor, and the ugly sticks. Unfortunately there hadn't been enough time for Tueen to use her magical horns to cure the ugly stick curse.

Chapter 16
Gil, Evets, and Begget

The journey through the jungle was dreamlike for Avry; he slipped in and out of consciousness only to hear his siblings' voices. "Avry, are you there?" Trueman whispered one of the times.

Avry's eyes fluttered open and then closed within the same split second.

"I hope he's alright," Caitlyn said.

"What did they do to him? Taylor, is that you? I can't understand you," Emelia called out.

"Avry, wake up! Are you there?" Trueman's squeaky voice trailed off.

Avry couldn't respond, and neither could Sir Taylor, with his mouth covered with black tar. All that could be heard was the angry murmur of a brave knight.

Avry struggled to open his eyes when he heard the heavy breathing of the trottles. The creatures didn't talk, they just gargled and moved swiftly though the thick of the woods.

Avry fainted at the sound of rustling brush and snapping twigs and didn't wake for the rest of the journey.

It was almost nightfall, and the trottles had reached a large stone tower that reached into the sky; they climbed into a large door and proceeded up to the top of the tower. Higher they climbed, never stopping once; the helpless Treelanders were at the mercy of Kildane's evil creations.

Inside the tower, a large copper bell hung from its peak and rang steadily every few seconds, maybe to signal that the Treelanders had arrived—no matter what the occasion, it was deafening, as it echoed down the tower.

When they arrived at the top of the tower, five elves carrying shackles and chains stood in a gigantic entrance that opened up to a huge, golden bridge. The long, wide, golden bridge was big enough for King Oliver's castle to fit on as well as Treeland village.

The trottles dropped Avry, Taylor, and the bags containing the ugly sticks onto the hard concrete. The mutant creatures turned around and left immediately down the long spiral stairs.

"Hold still for Waddle, you measly little man," an elf said, struggling to hold onto Taylor.

Pica, the head elf, had pointy ears and only a few hairs on his head. He pointed to Waddle and the other elves as he spoke. "Quick, get the young one, chain him while he's asleep."

"Yes, Pica, we hear you, no need to shout," Waddle said.

The elves all had long, pointed noses and beady, black eyes. Their bodies were short and fat and sat on top of long, meek, shaky legs. They scurried about quickly to shackle and chain Avry and Taylor's hands and feet. Then the elves proceeded to drag them across the golden bridge. Taylor's eyes opened wide at the sight of the giants' golden castle—bigger and brighter than he had expected—that stood at the end of the bridge.

Avry slowly opened his eyes and lifted his face off the cold, concrete floor. He was completely surrounded by metal bars. The Treelander shivered while he looked around the enormous room. The cage that contained him and Sir Taylor sat on a large table in the middle of the giants' kitchen. Their surroundings were magnified three times larger than Avry and Taylor.

Practically everything was made of gold, even the large bowls that sat on the table next to them. The room was dimly lit by a circle of candles that melted onto the scarred, wooden table. "*Odd that it isn't gold as well,*" Avry thought. On the far end of the table there were stacks of furniture made of gold, only this furniture was fit for someone the size of Avry.

Two elves entered the room, abruptly carrying a small box full of gold jewelry. They put it next to the small furniture on the table and then climbed down a small stairway that led from the table. The elves wasted no time and exited the room.

Sir Taylor sat quietly in the corner of the cage and smiled when he realized Avry was awake, "I was worried about you, Sir Avry."

"I'm not sure if it was the smell or the sight of the trottles that made me faint."

"Perhaps it was both."

"Yeah, I guess," Avry said as he looked around. Suddenly he gasped, "What did they do with the sticks and our stuff?"

"They are on the other side of the room hanging on the wall. They look safe for now."

The ugly sticks indeed sat quietly in Avry's backpack that hung from a gold hook on the giant wall beside the kitchen table. Trueman, Caitlyn, and Emelia had been silent since they entered the giant's castle.

Avry pounded the heel of his hand on the floor and shouted, "All this way, and now we are prisoners to the giants!"

"Don't worry lad, we will get out of here, have faith."

"Where we sit right now, it's hard to have any faith."

"Young man…two days ago I was trapped inside my sword—a prison that I suffered for a long time. You must stay positive."

"I'm trying, but we don't even know what happened to the egg," Avry whined.

"Oh, yes, we do…look!" Taylor pointed up to his left.

Perched high on a windowsill, sitting in a bed of hay, the beautiful dragon egg lay resting.

Avry began to laugh, "Is that who I think it is?"

"It's a funny sight, isn't it, lad?" Taylor snickered.

A familiar face, a thief, the dreaded sea monkey, Raider was chained to the wall and forced to sit on the dragon egg perhaps until it hatched.

"Hey Raider, are you practicing to be a mommy!" Avry taunted.

"When I get out of here, you little twerp, I'm coming after you!" Raider replied with his fist in the air.

"Well, I guess you got your wish," Avry called back. "You look so natural sitting up the on that egg. Look, its Raider, the dragon mommy!"

"My reward was going to be the biggest yet, until you messed everything up, you tree-brain!" Raider barked.

"You had no business coming to our land in the first place."

"Sir Avry, it is no point arguing with a scoundrel like Raider," Taylor said, shaking his head.

Avry nodded, "You're right. Thanks. I guess we have to find a way out of here—"

Without warning something shook the kitchen table.

"D-did you feel that?" Avry asked, looking around.

Taylor took a deep breath, "Yes, and I feel it's getting stronger, and louder. We best think of something and quick—"

A loud thunderous BANG came from behind the huge double- door entrance of the kitchen. Avry and Taylor were tossed about in the cage. They looked like rolling tumbleweeds as the floor shook with each rumble of seismic proportion. Raider screeched and began to tremble as the doors crashed open.

"Quiet down, little monkey bird," one giant shouted.

The giant's deep voice projected into the room like one hundred men talking at the same time. The giants' feet were so heavy that pictures on the wall turned crooked, and a glass jar vibrated onto the floor with a SMASH.

“More burlybeast, Gil, we need more!” the giant demanded.

“Evets told us she would cook us some more. She’s bringing a bundle up from the dungeon right now, Begget.”

“But I want more now!” Begget whined and smashed his fist on the table, just inches from the cage. The small jail knocked over on its side. Avry and Taylor hollered and grunted helplessly.

The two giant brothers, Begget and Gil, sat at table and stared into the cage. Gil’s round pudgy fingers lifted the cage back to its upright position.

Their protruding foreheads and big droopy eyes were enough to cause Avry to hide behind Taylor. But what made the giants even scarier looking was their lack of ears—they had no ears, just three slits like fish gills on the sides of their bald heads.

Suddenly, one of the walls began to move, the slow grinding stone against stone shook the floor as the wall slid open revealing a huge room below. A long marble staircase lead down into the enormous room, steam hissed and shot up into the air, you could hear the clanging of hammers and voices that echoed off the walls. Then, standing at the top of the stairs, was a large, obese, giant woman. She looked just like Gil and Begget, except she had long, frizzy, black hair that probably had never seen a comb. In her hand she carried a basket full of dead burlybeast ready to be cooked.

Evets shot a look at her brothers. Her stiff upper lip and scowled face was a good indication that she was in no mood to deal with their bickering. She said, "My beautiful castle is no place for an elves' workshop!"

"Sorry, sis, but it was the only place we could find to make the gold."

"It's bad enough that I had to go down two flights of stairs, around the huge pots of melted gold, through all the working elves, and step over the piles of produced gold merchandise to get your food, but on top of it all, I have to cook it!"

"But, sis..." the bothers said in unison.

Evets threw down the basket full of dead burlybeast in front of her brothers and continued to bicker, "And you have the nerve to complain how hungry you are! I heard you from all the way downstairs. I want my castle back in order...do you hear me?"

"We just love burlybeast. It's always best when you cook it," Gil said complimentarily. His big lip turned up to a goofy smile.

"WHEN I cook it!" Evets stammered. "I'm the only one who cooks around here! You two eat so much that we are going to have to make a bigger castle for those bellies of yours."

"Maybe we can just snack on these two humans in the cage." Begget snickered.

Avry let out a gasp and then crouched behind Taylor again.

"I don't think that would be a wise move, my big friends," Taylor said. His voice sounded tinny and meek to the giants.

"Yeah, or maybe we can split the sea monkey between us, Begget," Gil laughed.

"There will be no such happenings...at least not today!" Evets barked.

Raider looked relieved as he continued to sit on the dragon egg. He shrilled at the thought of being an afternoon snack, and he was glad that one of the giants was not hungry for sea monkeys.

Evets placed the burlybeast into a large brick oven that burned hot and bright, while Begget stared with excitement and licked his lips.

Gil was preoccupied with another idea, "Hey, Evets, can we cook the dragon egg for breakfast?"

SLAM!

Evets hammered a large wooden club, just inches from Gil's hand on the table.

"Not yet! Enough with the requests, don't you boys have something you should be doing?"

Avry stood up, clutched the cage bars with his hands, cleared his throat, and looked right into the eyes of the giants, "Why do you hate my people and the dragons so much?"

Evets walked closer to the cage, her eyes squinted, her face red with anger, and gazed deeply into Avry's brown eyes. She said, "It was one of you puny pests that turned the dragons against us giants."

"I don't believe that, not for a minute. Our people are peaceful," Avry said.

"Believe it or not, but it was your very own King Oliver himself that cast such an evil act."

"Imposturous!" Taylor shouted, "The king would do no such thing!"

"Is that why you abducted the king?" Avry asked.

"Master Kildane took the king," Gil replied.

"Quiet down, Gil!" Evets commanded.

Avry pushed his face closer to the steel bars, and asked, "Why do you guys help Kildane?"

"Master Kildane promised us he would rid the land of all the dragons, and in return we help him make all his golden treasures," Evets replied.

"Yeah, and then we can get rid of you puny people and have all the burlybeast we want," Begget snorted.

Avry stuck out his chest, crossed his arms, and looked at the giants with pride, saying, "Well, for your information, Kildane is dead. I killed him myself!"

The giants began to laugh in disbelief, their big bellies shook up and down, and they pounded the table with their huge fists.

Outside, the rain began to beat down hard on the roof, lightning crashed through the sky, and thunder shook the castle.

"Why are you laughing?" Avry tried to talk, but the giants were laughing so hard they couldn't hear him. "It's true..." he tried to continue.

Taylor looked over Avry's shoulder while he tried to talk to the giants; his eyes were fixed on a figure that stood at the end of the table. Avry caught Taylor's stare and turned quickly to find out what was hypnotizing him.

Chapter 17
The Man behind the Mask

A dark, hooded figure walked in the shadows at the far end of the table. He walked with a limp and carried a shiny object in his hands. He cast shadows onto the walls as he approached. Lightning flashed into the room and quickly revealed the face of a very familiar man. Cold chills ran up Avry's spine, his face turned white, and his jaw hung open.

Did Avry's eyes deceive him?

Was he looking into the face of a ghost or perhaps he bumped his head and was dreaming. The dream-demon had returned. This was the vision that he could not remember—the one that haunted him for months, and now everything came into view. The image became clearer when the man with the black mask walked by the bright candles that lit the table closest to the cage.

Kildane had survived the fall into the bottomless pit; his arm was replaced with a new one made of gold. He laughed hysterically at the shocked expressions on Taylor and Avry's faces, "Trapped like a rat, I see. Now that I have you, you will witness the power of a great warlock."

Sir Taylor paced back and forth while Kildane approach them. "Don't you think you've done enough damage to the land of Epalushia? Everywhere you've been is now plagued with some sort of curse or destruction."

“Yeah...and what about the bottomless pit? I thought you were dead,” Avry shook his head.

Kildane walked directly up to the cage, his evil eyes peering out of two slits in the shiny black mask. He taunted, “Yes, yes, yes. Things don’t appear as they seem, do they? That pit leads to a dungeon in this very castle. My plan was going so well, until you and your brother interfered. Raider was going to steal the egg, regardless of who interfered, however, I did not plan on having anyone chasing him through the forbidden land. So I watched closely, and made sure that Raider made it here safely with the precious egg.”

Without thinking, Avry ran up to the cage bars, and stood face to face with Kildane, shouting, “That dragon egg belongs to us, and we are not going to let anyone harm it!”

Kildane reached into the cage and shoved Avry back, “Quiet! I have the egg now, and we will train the newborn dragon to like the giants and hate the puny humans.”

The giants began to laugh again when Avry barked in, “How is it that you watched us? Were you the one following us?”

Kildane reached into his robe, pulled out a roll of parchment tied by a red string, and held it toward the cage, “This, my friend is the key to everything.”

“The starlight map belongs to me. It was a gift from King Oliver!” Avry spat.

“It was I who planted the map in the King’s throne room with a note to give it to you for your journey. That stupid king had no idea of the power of this map," Kildane said, as he held the map up high.

"And where is the king? What have you done with him?" Taylor asked.

"Ah, so noble, young knight. However, at last, the king is dead," Kildane cackled.

Taylor leaped at Kildane and tried to reach him through the bars, but was unsuccessful. "Why...you...scoundrel," he snarled.

Kildane silenced Taylor's scream with his cold, golden, lifeless hand.

Avry stood calm, trying to think of a plan, and still remained curious about the map, and asked, "So why is the map so powerful? What is the third use?"

Kildane pushed Taylor backward and pulled out the lumpy rock that hung on his gold necklace. He held the map and the rock next to each other and said, "With this map and this rock, you can do amazing things. While you had the map, I was able to see your every step through the rock, but that's not all. The map only allowed you to track where you had traveled, and see great distances or things that were hidden."

So what else does that stupid rock do?" Avry asked.

"This is the starlight rock. Together with the map, it will show you the complete detailed map of Epalushia; and it allows you to transport to anywhere you want just by pointing the rock to your destination on the map. The starlight rock contains great power...great power."

"Very clever, but as long as I'm alive, I still serve the Kingdom of Epalushia and New Gander, and I will not allow you to get away with this!" Taylor shouted as he raised his fists.

Begget's large hands reached over and grabbed the cage; he picked it up and put it close to his large mouth. His breathe was hot and smelly when he said, "You *is* too puny and stuck in this cage. How is it that you will stop us?"

Gil licked his hungry lips with excitement as the cage passed his face. He groaned, "Let's eat them now, my belly can't wait!"

A silver spark shot out of Kildane's golden arm and singed Gil on his nose. Gil stood cross-eyed as he looked at his giant snout that was charred and smoking.

"Put them down, you big oaf!" Kildane commanded.

Petrified as they were, Avry and Taylor still managed to laugh at the sight of the zapped giant.

"Perhaps they will end up killing each other, before they get to us," Taylor snickered.

Avry's face became serious, and he pleaded to Kildane and the giants once more. "There are others besides us, we are not alone, and soon you will pay!"

"Nonsense, you tree-twerp. In a few minutes the dragon egg will hatch, and I will rule the entire land of Epalushia!" Kildane said as he began to pace.

The hairs on Avry's neck stood straight up as the castle became deathly quiet. The elves' workshop was silent, only the hisses of steam and the gurgling sound of bubbles remained. The giants looked at each other, dumbfounded.

Kildane walked cautiously to the large marble staircase that led down to the huge room below. "I don't believe I told anyone that they could have a break. Why aren't they working—"

From outside the castle wall, a terrifying screech had alarmed everyone. Outside the windows, hot flames splattered against the glass followed by an enormous *CRASH*. The room rumbled, as the concrete wall exploded inward. Cold air rushed in through the enormous hole in the wall. Evets caught the dragon egg in midair before it crashed to the floor. Raider fell to the ground, and his chains broke free from the concrete, rocks toppled onto Kildane, the cage plummeted to the floor and snapped open, and dust settled to the ground, leaving everyone ghostly white.

Hidden within the smoke, loud strokes of two large wings flapped violently. The large fleshy wings fluttered rapidly, blowing clouds of dust into spiral funnels. The dust began to settle, and the fierce creature appeared out of the cloud. Willow sat valiantly on the back of Jewlz, the dragon. Her eyes were fearless, and she pointed her sword toward the giants as she charged forward.

More strange and unusual sounds came from the elves' workshop and grew louder with every second that passed. Prince William sat proudly on the two-headed unicorn; they emerged from the room below along with the enslaved elves that the prince had set free.

Haooone!

Haooone!

A horn sounded twice. Tueen's magical horns had released the healing powers to free the Treelanders from the ugly stick curse.

Trueman, Caitlyn, and Emelia sprang to life out of Avry's backpack; they grabbed their weapons and joined Prince William in his battle against the giants.

"Oh my god, it's the prince! Quick, Emelia, how does my hair look?" Caitlyn asked.

"Who cares?" Emelia sniffed deeply. "Smell that burlybeast cooking—I'm hungry!"

"Just get the giants before they eat us," Trueman griped.

Gil and Begget swatted away elves that attacked their feet. A group of elves carried a large rope and tried to trip the giants, while other elves jabbed them with knives, sticks, and anything that would cause them great pain.

Price William flew passed Gil and jabbed him in the eye, while Trueman spiked his sword in the giant's leg. Gil fell hard and fast to the ground and shook the castle floor.

"Good shot, Trueman!" Prince William cheered.

Caitlyn climbed up Begget's back, while he struggled to untie his feet that the elves had bound. She jabbed her sword into his big head, and then jumped off the giant, who squirmed in pain.

Tueen and the Prince flew underneath Caitlyn, as she fell to the floor. Caitlyn landed in Prince William's arms, and he held her tight.

"Thanks," Caitlyn said with a huge smile and flush cheeks.

Prince William just smiled back and was lost for words.

Fire spewed out of the dragon's mouth and burned Evets's arms. The pain caused her to drop the egg. "Avry—Quick! Catch the egg!" Willow shouted.

Avry and Taylor ran toward the egg and caught it before it hit the concrete floor; it slipped out of their hands and rolled across the room toward the large marble staircase.

Avry's heart almost stopped. He yelled to Taylor while he chased after the rolling egg, "You help the others with the giants, while I get the egg!"

Avry's path was suddenly blocked when Kildane emerged from the rubble; his black mask had broken half way off and exposed the mysterious face of the warlock.

"Demobilopis!" Kildane said, his spell stopping the egg in its tracks. "HA, HA, HA! I told you that you were no match for the great Kildane."

Avry began to panic when he looked upon Kildane's face for the first time. He said, "K-King Oliver! I can see your face. Snap out of it! What has happened to you?"

Avry's words halted the fight in the giants' kitchen; silence fell on the castle, and everyone stared in amazement at the true identity of the man behind the mask.

Gasps and whispers could be heard, as Avry slowly approached Kildane, and asked, "Why? King Oliver, please tell me, why? Why have you done this to our beautiful land?"

"Power and gold, Avry!" the warlock grunted.

"It's more like greed. You're the king of Epalushia; you have everything that you want, why would you want more?" Avry asked furiously.

"Not true Avry...you see...the queen had fallen in love with my brother Arthur, and he needed to be stopped. Everyone began moving to New Gander to live under the rule of my brother, and I couldn't have that."

"So you stopped it all with the ugly stick curse, you traitor," Taylor yelled.

Kildane/King Oliver continued, "When the people fled back to my kingdom from New Gander, they knew it was the only safe place. Turning the dragons on the giants and bringing the pirates, fairies, and leprechauns was all part of my plan to rule the land. But then you—you stupid Treelanders came along and messed up everything."

The giants began to move closer to Kildane, Avry, and Taylor. "You tricked us," Evets droning voice echoed through the room. "You turned the dragons on my father and the rest of the giants, and now they're dead and gone."

Tueen flew Prince William and Caitlyn over to the man known as King Oliver. The prince slowly walked over to his father with a sulky face, and pleaded, "Father...the rock, please, give it to me now! You told me that you had gotten rid of that evil stone."

"I will never part with this!" Kildane/King Oliver growled.

Beams of electricity shot out of the starlight rock

and immobilized everyone in the room; ghost owls emerged from the elves' workshop and picked the elves up into the air, while Kildane ran for the dragon egg.

"I can't move my body!" Taylor grunted.

"Neither...can...I..." Prince William said, struggling desperately.

Jewlz began to howl, as she watched Kildane pick up the egg while she hovered, frozen in midair.

Avry looked down at the sword in his hands—Sir Taylor's sword of the knight. It illuminated into a bright purple light, and the warlock's electricity seemed to have had no effect on it. Avry felt something strange and mysterious happen while he held the mighty sword—his hands felt stronger, and he was able to move slightly from side to side until the sword broke the electrical current that held Avry in place. Avry charged through the room and held the sword up to the warlock's electrical force field. The room full of captives had been released immediately.

Avry reflected the electricity off the magical steel blade and onto the ghost owls. The owls vanished immediately when the electrical beam connected with each one of them.

With the ghost owls gone, Kildane/King Oliver began to run down the marble staircase into the elves' work shop. The dragon, with Willow on her back, chased after the warlock. Avry and the others followed closely behind.

Kildane clutched the egg in the crook of one arm (his good one), and clenched the starlight map between his teeth. He climbed drunkenly up a tall ladder. The ladder stood almost one hundred feet high and led to the top of a huge melting pot. Avry climbed without a care in the world and was only a few steps behind Kildane.

Jewlz lunged at Kildane and almost knocked him off the ladder. She circled back while the warlock fumbled to regain his grip. Kildane reached with his free hand and grabbed at the open air, he swung backward while the egg bounced in his arm several times. Kildane regained his balance and began to climb higher.

Helpless and desperate, Kildane screamed to the angry mob, "Stop now or I will drop the egg!" He held the dragon egg over the hot melted gold that bubbled below.

Everyone in the room gasped. Avry's heart hammered in his chest.

Jewlz darted after the egg again, and Willow held tightly around her neck. The dragon's wing struck Kildane/King Oliver and sent the egg flying into the air. Kildane fell over the edge of the pot, and Avry held the tail of his robe.

Meanwhile, Willow grabbed the falling egg and cradled it tightly in her arms as she and the dragon crashed to the floor below.

Kildane slipped into the melting pot. Avry clawed and grabbed onto him but was only able to grasp the starlight rock that was connected to the warlock's gold necklace.

Avry looked at the dangling warlock with a tense face and said, "I could let you go and kill you for good...but something just won't let me."

"Kildane struggled to speak, "Maybe...if I let go...of...the... map—"

Avry screamed as he watched the map fall into the burning pot of gold, he felt his hands begin to burn while he held the starlight rock, and then just inches before the map made contact with the molten pit, it disappeared.

"King Oliver, I can't hold on!" Avry cried desperately. He felt the necklace slipping through his sweaty palms.

"Not...King Oliver...Kildane.You must come with me!" Kildane laughed and cackled wildly like a possessed hyena.

Ghost owls emerged out of the golden pot and grabbed onto Kildane and Avry. Avry pulled back with all his might while the owls yanked them downward; his feet slipped off the landing that held him in place, and they plummeted into burning molten pot. The heat engulfed them instantly, and Avry hollered helplessly.

The room full of friends and foe gasped once more as something strange and unexpected happened—

Avry had stopped with a jolt in midair. He was amazed to find himself in the clutches of an enormous giant hand—Evets's hand.

Avry watched as Kildane dangled below him—hanging only by the gold necklace—he held firmly to the starlight rock in both his hands.

Evets pulled Avry up out of the pot, and the warlock clung for dear life. The warlock's feet peddled the hot open air, and the ghost owls tried to take hold. Avry tugged the magic rock and tried to pull Kildane up with him; beads of sweat covered his body, his muscles flexed and twitched, and the warlock began to rise with him.

The chain links on the necklace stretched with every inch that they rose. Suddenly there was a *plink* sound, and then one of the links broke open. Kildane clutched tightly to the broken link, slipping with every heartbeat. There were two last sounds that echoed in Avry's head for some months after.

Snap!

Zip!

The necklace broke, and Kildane plunged into the burning pot of gold.

The ghost owls disappeared when Kildane splashed into the scalding, gold liquid—he burned orange, melted blue, and vaporized. A ghostly white cloud exploded into the air and fizzled into nothingness.

Avry gave a sigh of relief as he looked up at Evets with her big droopy eyes, "Thanks," he said with a smile. He swallowed back the lump in his throat.

Evets placed Avry down gently on the ground. He ran quickly over to the dragon that lay still on the floor. Jewlz's breathing was heavy, and she could barely keep her big eyes open. Willow held the dragon egg in front of Jewlz; it cracked suddenly from top to bottom and then split open. The young baby dragon wobbled out of the cracked shell, flapped its tender, red wings, and let out the smallest squeak.

Jewlz smiled, her eyes softened, she took one last breath and then shut her eyes, never to open them again.

Willow was crouched on the floor and crying when Avry and the others approached her. No one in the room spoke. They bowed their heads, as the Treelanders huddled around Jewlz and the newborn dragon. Tears flowed down their faces as they embraced in a hug and watched the baby cuddle with its mother for the first and last time.

Chapter 18
The Return to Treeland

The giants and elves stood by and watched as the Treelanders reunited—not since their first encounter with Captain Slaughter had they all been together. The fact that they were still surrounded by elves, giants, and large pots of melted gold didn't bother them. The large machines in the elves' workshop no longer hissed and puffed. The room was replaced with cries and laughter.

"It's good to see you, sis," Avry said.

"It's good to see you all," Willow sobbed. "I love you and missed you so much." She wiped the tears of joy that trickled down her cheeks.

Prince William turned to Caitlyn and gave her an unexpected kiss on the cheek. Caitlyn blushed crimson.

"I wish I didn't see that," Trueman moaned loudly.

The room began to laugh at Trueman's comment.

"Can we eat now?" Emelia said with a smirk and a shrug of her shoulders.

Avry nodded, and said, "For once Emelia, I'll have to agree...let's go home, guys."

Emelia became startled as she looked around the room, "Hey! Where's Raider?"

"I'm afraid he has escaped once again, my dear," Taylor said disappointedly.

Avry's face became scarlet, and he erupted, "Man I hate that sea monkey—HEY!" Something fell from the ceiling and bonked Avry on the head. "Look! It's the map!" He said. He looked up, as a scraggly yellow feather floated from the ceiling and landed on his nose.

"Spikey?" Avry called curiously.

"That was weird," Trueman said.

The rolled up parchment was still intact, the red ribbon was neatly tied as it was when Avry used it all along their journey to the giants.

There was no logical explanation how the map landed back in Avry's hands, perhaps it just found its way to its rightful owner—nevertheless, the starlight map and the rock were all they needed to get back home.

The elves were free to go home, as the giants had no use for them, no more gold to make, and no more Kildane to torture them.

The giants thanked the Treelanders for eliminating Kildane, and promised to leave them alone as long as they sent a cartload of burlybeast each week. The Treelanders agreed and hoped that they all could live in peace and harmony.

Prince William and Caitlyn decided to fly to New Gander with Tueen to free the ugly stick curse.

"See you back at Treeland, Cait," Willow said sheepishly.

Caitlyn and Prince William waved good-bye, as Tueen flew gracefully into the air and raced off to New Gander through the hole in the kitchen wall.

The others said their good-byes and then

gathered around Jewlz and her baby. Avry laughed at Trueman who was trying to carry all their backpacks, "You got it all, Trueman?"

Trueman heaved the backpacks over his shoulder, "Ahrrrrrrrg...Got it!" he moaned.

"Even the swamp water?" Avry asked knowingly.

"Even the swamp water," Trueman said, cracking a smile.

"Okay then, here we go," said Avry. He had no idea what to expect as he, Willow, Trueman, Emelia, and Taylor held hands around the dragons. Avry opened the map, this time the parchment was not black, it had a complete, detailed layout of Epalushia.

Avry pointed the starlight rock at the image of Treeland—flashes of light swirled around them like a giant tornado, faster and faster it turned, until they vanished from the giants' castle.

The early morning sun had just touched the lake below the falls where Zita, Zia, and Spikey watched anxiously for the Treelanders' arrival. The bright-light tornado transporter had set down on the bank of Sky Lake; within seconds Jewlz's lifeless body floated into the air and vanished into the great falls.

The newborn dragon frolicked in the lake while the Zita, Zia, and Spikey greeted the Treelanders and Taylor.

"No time for chit chattin' with me," Zia cried, "I have a potion to finish. Quick, give me the swamp water!"

Trueman reached into Avry's backpack and

handed the old brown potion bottle to Zia. The hunched-over witch all dressed in white took to her broom and flew off to Treeland with her potion.

"Don't worry...you will get a chance to say hello to Zia later," Zita laughed.

"Zita, do you really think Zia can cure our village?" Emelia asked.

"Young lady, not only will they be cured when you arrive at home, they will be unharmed as if nothing ever happened."

Zita gave Taylor a firm handshake, grinned from ear to ear, and said, "I see you still have the sword that I made for you some time ago."

"Zita, my old friend," Taylor said, patting the wizard on his shoulder. "I can't thank you enough for this amazing gift. However, I think that Avry has earned the right to keep this sword."

Avry's eyes opened wide as Taylor gave him the sword of the knight. He said, "Wow...It's mine? I really can keep it?"

"Take care of it because you never know when you're going to run into another evil warlock," Sir Taylor said, ruffling his hair.

"Zita, there's something that I have wondered for a while now," Avry said, looking curiously at the wizard.

"What's that, young man?"

"Why did Kildane fear this sword?" he asked as held up the shining metal blade.

Zita put his hand over his heart, saying, "The heart of this sword is lined with strongest powers that will defeat any warlock."

Avry shrugged his shoulders in confusion, and asked, "What kind of powers?"

"The strongest power of all—peace, love, and harmony," Zita said, pulling Avry and Trueman aside and giving them a hug. His smile became somber as he looked into the boys eyes. "Please enlighten an old wizard. I attest you boys have learned a valuable lesson."

Trueman looked up to the empty nest that still sat on the side of the cliff near the great falls and said, "I know one thing—never take something that doesn't belong to you. It can only lead to trouble."

"Ah, yes, true," Zita smirked. "And you, Avry, did you get anything out of your adventure?"

Avry smiled as he watched Willow and the baby dragon splashing in the lake. He replied, "I don't think you need to have great power and good fortune to truly be happy. King Oliver had everything he wanted and still he wanted more. I guess greed can really kill a man's soul."

Emelia stood by and eavesdropped while she ate chocolate ferns that grew by the lake. She added, "Yeah, and to think, the king will never get to eat anything as good as this ever again."

Everyone laughed, and then drew their attention to the baby dragon as it snapped her head back out of the water and proudly showed two fish and gold flakes that she caught with her teeth.

"I think perhawps we should cawll her Lucky," Spikey squawked.

"Her? It's not a he?" Trueman asked.

“Yes, Trueman, the dragon is a girl,” Zita replied.

“I think Lucky suits her well,” Taylor grinned.

“I think she likes it too,” Willow shouted gleefully.

Lucky enjoyed her new home in the small cove under the great falls. It was, after all, where her mother grew up, and there was no place finer than Sky Lake.

“I’ll look after Lucky,” Zita said. “You should go. I’m sure by now Zia has used her beautiful witchcraft.”

Zita stayed behind with Lucky at Sky Lake, while the others raced off to Treeland.

The fresh scent of pine needles tickled Avry’s nose when they arrived at Treeland. The tall, green pine trees swayed in the breeze and gave way to the wooden village high above. Avry, Trueman, Willow, and Emelia climbed expediently to see the long-awaited site of their family and friends. Zia flew down on her broom and gave Sir Taylor a ride to join the festivities with the Treelanders.

Riding high on the back of the two-headed unicorn, Caitlyn and Prince William yelled with joy at the cheering villagers below. Tueen blew her horns and touched down on the main street of Treeland.

No longer under the spell of the gargoyle, their flaming statue bodies had returned to normal; Zia’s magic potion had truly worked; and there were tears, laughs, and hugs all around. The overwhelming reunion of family and friends led to a grand celebration for the entire land of Epalushia.

Later that night, the celebration still echoed through the trees as the exhausted Treelanders rested in their beds. Willow, Emelia, and Caitlyn were sound asleep when their mother, Lorri, looked in on them; she covered the jars of fireflies to dim the room, and then climbed over to the boys' hut.

Inside the boys cluttered bedroom, Avry and Trueman swayed in their hammocks while Spikey Bluejeans listened to the stories about Kildane and the giants. The boys were startled for a minute when their mother entered the room.

"Oh…hi, Mom," Trueman grinned.

"Are you two still awake?" she asked knowingly. "I would have guessed that you were sound asleep like your sisters."

"But, Mom, Spikey's here, and there's so much to tell," Trueman pleaded.

"Well, you better get some rest. We have to begin preparations for Caitlyn's wedding starting as early as tomorrow."

Avry yawned and smiled at his mom, and said, "Okay Mum…more burlybeasts to hunt tomorrow, I gather?"

"That's right, and this time, no wondering off."

"Don't worry, Mom, I'm not afraid of those silly burlybeasts anymore," Trueman said fiercely.

"Goodnight boys," she said, exiting the room.

"HEY—Mum!" Avry called out.

Lorri poked her head back through a window and said, "What's that Avry?"

Avry sat up with a huge smile, and replied, "It's good to be home again."

Lorri was overwhelmed with tears of joy and just blew the boys a kiss goodnight. She turned away and then turned back again clearing her throat, "Goodnight boys. Oh, and Spikey—don't keep my boys awake all night."

Spikey squawked as she walked off.

As soon their mother's footsteps died out, the tattered, yellow- haired bird with blue jeans continued to pace back and forth on the windowsill. Trueman had not let that affect him; he snored so loudly that Avry thought it would wake up the whole village.

Avry tried to avoid the sound of Spikey's long nails that tapped the bamboo sill while he paced. He attempted to silence Trueman's snoring by throwing pillows at his head. He even tried to cover his ears with two pillows, but nothing had irked him more than the sharp sound of Spikey's whistling.

"Okay, why are you keeping me awake?" Avry moaned.

"Yaw didn't finish the story!"

"But Spikey...there's so much to tell, I mean, we were gone for a whole week, and besides, you know how the story ends."

Spikey shook his tail feathers, flew over next to Avry, and squawked, "Just tell me wan quick story before you go to sleep."

"Alright...fine, but first, you need to answer a question for me."

Spikey just shook his head and squawked in agreement.

Avry smirked at Spikey as he pulled a tattered yellow feather from his shirt pocket, "So tell me how you got the starlight map and returned it without anyone seeing you."

"Waasn't me," Spikey squawked.

"Well, if it wasn't you, who could it have been?"

"Perhawps it was the magic of a wizard."

"Zita? Are you saying Zita was there? It can't be possible. Your feather floated down from the giants' castle ceiling along with the map. Now how do you explain that?"

"Maybe, it was someone much closer to the starlight map, other than Zita."

"Me!?" Avry shouted. "Are you saying I did it?"

"Could be...secrets of the wizards yaw know."

Avry grew silent and thought for a moment.

To think, that maybe he might have the powers of a wizard, or how is it that a normal boy from Treeland could do such a thing; and what was the true power of the starlight rock?

Maybe he would never really know. However, Avry was growing tired, and he was glad to be back in his bed. Then one final thought occurred to Avry—the five siblings had witnessed so many magical things on their journey that anything could be possible in a land so mystical. He quickly sprang from his hammock, opened the wooden trunk where he kept his belongings, and took out a stack of parchment and an ink quill.

Spikey listened contently each night for two weeks as Avry told his story and wrote down each unbelievable chapter; when he was finished he added his story to the Tree of Life, and each night, as everyone from Treeland sat around the campfire, Avry, Trueman, Willow, Emelia, and Caitlyn each took a turn telling the amazing adventures of their journey to the giants.

About the Author

In 2006 Stephen self-published his first novel, *The Treelanders-Journey to the Giants*. Locally it was an instant success. He has attended over 30 schools in New England sharing his story with students and teachers. He won the i-Universe Publishers Choice and Editors Choice awards where his novel was found by Dailey Swan Publishing and its editors.

Stephen has 4 follow-up novels ready based on the Treelanders and a fifth in the works.

A sculptor and Musician, he lives in Hudson, Massachusetts with his family.

Other Titles fom Dailey Swan Publishing

Nogglestones by Wil Radcliffe
978-0-9773676-9-6 $14.95

Sorenson's Gift by Robin Roberts
978-0-9815845-7-7 $15.95

The Freddie Anderson Chroncilces
(Freddie Anderson's Home)
by John Ricks
978-0-9773676-7-2 $12.95

The Broomwhistle Chronicles
(The Witchhunt of the Dwills)
By Eric Dryer Smith
978-0-9824331-1-9 $12.95

www.daileyswanpublishing.com